THE WORLD OF
NORM
MAY CAUSE IRRITATION

Thanks again to my brilliant editor, Catherine.
Not that it needing edited.

ORCHARD BOOKS
338 Euston Road, London NW1 3BH
Orchard Books Australia
Level 17/207 Kent Street, Sydney, NSW 2000

First published in 2012 by Orchard Books

A Paperback Original

ISBN 978 1 408 31304 6

A CIP catalogue record for this book is available from the British Library.

13

Printed in Great Britain

Orchard Books is a division of Hachette Children's Books,
an Hachette UK company.

www.hachette.co.uk

JONATHAN MERES

THE WORLD OF
NORM
MAY CAUSE IRRITATION

ORCHARD

To Fiona – because I'm worth it.

CHAPTER 1

Norm knew it was going to be one of those days when he woke up and found himself standing at a supermarket checkout, totally naked.

"I'm afraid that's not allowed," said the checkout assistant.

"Pardon?" said Norm.

"It's strictly against the rules," said the assistant.

"What is?" said Norm. "Shopping without any clothes on?"

"No," said the assistant. "Having ten items in your basket. This checkout's nine items or less."

Norm did a quick count. Sure enough, there were ten items in the basket – every one of them the supermarket's own, cheaper brand.

"Sorry, I'll put one back," said Norm.

"It's too late for that," said the assistant.

"What?" said Norm, with a growing sense of disbelief.

"It's too late. I'm going to have to ask you to leave."

"Are you serious?" said Norm.

As if to demonstrate just how serious she was, the checkout assistant pushed a button and spoke into a microphone. "Security to checkout three, please – security to checkout three."

"But..." said Norm.

"Stand away from the till," said a strangely familiar sounding voice. "You have ten seconds to comply."

You have Ten seconds to COMPLY

Norm turned round to see a strangely familiar looking security guard approaching. "Dad? It's me! Norman!"

But Norm's dad took no notice. "Here, take this," he said, handing Norm a packet of own-brand coco pops and ushering him towards the exit.

"It's OK thanks, I'm not hungry," said Norm.

"Not to eat," said Norm's dad. "To cover up your..."

"Oh, right," said Norm, suddenly remembering he was butt naked.

What was going on? wondered Norm. And why was his dad dressed as a security guard? Was he going to a fancy dress party? If so then a security guard at a supermarket was a pretty rubbish thing to go as. Unless, of course, the theme of the party was supermarkets. Or security guards. And frankly neither seemed terribly likely.

"This way please," said Norm's dad officiously.

Cameras flashed as Norm was led from the store wearing nothing but a strategically placed packet of own-brand coco pops. A crowd had gathered to watch the unfolding drama and in the distance the wail of a police siren could be heard, getting louder and louder.

"All right, **Norman**?" said another strangely familiar sounding voice.

Norm looked round to see Chelsea, his occasional next-door neighbour, grinning from ear to ear. Worse still, she appeared to be filming proceedings with her phone. If things could actually *get* any more humiliating, they just *had*.

"I see you've only got a small packet," laughed Chelsea.

Norm could feel himself blushing.

"How could you do this to us, Norman?" said yet another familiar sounding voice.

It was Norm's mum. Next to her, Norm could see his middle brother, Brian, and next to Brian his youngest brother, Dave.

"You've brought shame on the whole family," said Norm's mum, gravely.

"No he hasn't," chirped Dave. "This is well funny, this is!"

"Shut up, Dave!" said Brian.

"Honestly, love, this is very embarrassing," said Norm's mum.

"It's not my fault, Mum!" protested Norm. "I didn't see any signs saying 'No naked shopping allowed'!"

"What?" said Norm's mum. "No, I meant it's very embarrassing you shopping in a place like this. We normally go to Tesco's. What on earth will the neighbours think?"

"Your mother's right, Norman," said Norm's dad. "Surely things aren't *that* bad, are they?"

Norm looked at his dad for a second. If it wasn't for him getting flipping sacked, none of this would have happened in the first flipping place.

"I dunno, Dad. *You* tell *me*!"

But before Norm's dad could reply, a police car screeched to a halt and a dog got out of the driver's door.

"You're under arrest on suspicion of having ten items at the nine items or less checkout," said the dog. "You have the right to remain silent. Anything you say may be taken down and used as evidence against you."

Norm chose to remain silent. The truth was Norm couldn't have said anything if he'd wanted to. He'd started to feel a bit woozy and light-headed. Like he was about to faint. Whether it was the shock of seeing a dog driving a police car, or a dog that could *talk* driving a police car, was hard to say.

"Norman?" said Norm's mum, as Norm's legs suddenly turned to jelly and he collapsed in a quivering heap on the floor.

CHAPTER 2

"Norman?" said Norm's mum again. "Time to wake up, love."

Norm grunted.

"Rise and shine," said Norm's mum, shaking Norm gently by the shoulder.

Norm still showed no sign of waking up.

"Time to get dressed."

That did the trick. Norm sat up in a flash.

"Where's my coco pops?" he said, thrashing about the bedclothes in a panic.

"What?" said his mum.

"The packet of coco pops!" said Norm. "I need it!"

"What for?"

Norm looked down and was mightily relieved to see that he was wearing pyjamas.

"Er, nothing."

"I think *someone's* been having a dream!" laughed Norm's mum.

Norm looked around him. Mountain-biking posters on the walls? Check. Pile of mountain-biking magazines on his bedside table? Check. Mountain-biking helmet hanging behind the door? Check.

"Is **this** a dream, Mum?"

"Pardon?"

"Is this a dream?" said Norm. "Maybe I'm **dreaming** that I'm dreaming."

Norm's mum smiled.

"Maybe *you're* dreaming, Mum," said Norm. "Maybe *I'm* in *your* dream! Maybe none of this is real."

"Or maybe you should just get up," said Norm's mum. "It's nearly ten o'clock!"

"I thought it was Saturday," said Norm.

"It is."

"So why do I have to get up?"

"Your cousins are coming, remember?"

"Aw, no!" wailed Norm.

Now Norm knew for sure this wasn't a dream. It was an

absolute-flipping-nightmare!

His cousins? His perfect flipping cousins? What did they have to come and ruin everything for?

"How long are they staying?"

"All day," said Norm's mum. "We're having lunch and then we're all going for a walk."

A **walk**? thought Norm. If there was one thing worse than spending time with his perfect cousins it was being forced to go on a flipping walk with them! Norm couldn't see the point of walks at the best of times. He did quite enough walking without ever actually *going* on one.

He **walked** to school.

He **walked** up and down the stairs.

He'd even been known to **walk** to the TV to change channels if he couldn't find the remote and his brothers weren't around to do it for him.

Walking was something you did to get from A to B in the shortest possible time, by the shortest possible route. Walking was most definitely *not* something you did for pleasure!

"You're not serious, Mum? A **walk**?"

"What's wrong with that, Norman?"

"What's *right* with it, you mean!"

"Now, now, don't be like that."

Norm had a thought. There was one way of making the experience at least vaguely bearable.

"Can I bring my bike?"

"No, you can't bring your bike! We're going on a *walk*!"

Norm sighed with resignation. Short of being struck down by an incurable tropical disease, he knew that there was very little chance of getting out of this.

"Oh, come on, Norman," said Norm's mum. "They're not that bad, are they?"

Bad? thought Norm. His cousins were worse than bad, with their perfect teeth and their perfect hair and their perfect manners. Always banging on about playing some random instrument in some stupid concert, or going to some country Norm had never even heard of. *They* hadn't had to move to a smaller house because they were skint! If *they'd* been forced to eat own-brand coco pops they'd have been straight on the phone to flipping Childline!

"Oh, and open the window before you come down, love," said Norm's mum, disappearing through the doorway. "It smells awful in here."

"Yeah, so?" muttered Norm under his breath.

"Your cousins are coming!" said Norm's mum, whose hearing was a lot better than Norm thought it was.

"And I suppose **they** never fart," said Norm.

"Just do it please, love," shouted Norm's mum.

Norm grudgingly got out of bed and opened the window. Knowing his perfect cousins, they probably **didn't** fart. And even if they **did**, they probably smelt of flipping flowers or something.

Norm glanced outside. It looked like it was about to pee it down with rain. The sky was the colour of...of...actually, Norm couldn't think what the sky was the colour of. No doubt his perfect cousins would be able to though. In fact, knowing his perfect cousins they'd probably write a flipping poem about it. Without even being told to!

Flipping freaks of nature, thought Norm, trudging wearily towards the stairs.

CHAPTER 3

"Hey, Norman!" said Dave as Norm appeared in the kitchen. "Where are your coco pops?"

Dave and Brian both fell about laughing. Norm glared at his mum.

"Sorry, love," said Norm's mum. "But you have to admit, it *was* pretty funny."

"Glad you think so," said Norm, huffily.

Norm looked outside. By now it had actually started to rain. The question was how bad did the rain have to get before the walk got called off? A short, sharp shower? A torrential downpour? A full-on tropical storm? Even then it might not be enough, thought Norm, though at least there'd be a chance of being struck by lightning, which was infinitely preferable to spending more time with his perfect cousins.

"So, what was the dream about?" said Norm's dad. "Apart from coco pops."

"Oh, you know," said Norm.

"No, I don't," said Norm's dad. "That's why I'm asking."

"Just, you know – stuff," said Norm.

"Stuff?"

Norm nodded.

"What kind of stuff?"

Norm thought for a moment. He didn't need to go into *too* much detail, did he?

"I was in a supermarket."

"Yeah?" said Norm's dad. "And?"

"I got thrown out."

"What for?"

"For being in the nine items or less queue with ten items."

"That was it?" said Norm's dad. "Nothing else?"

"Nothing else," said Norm.

"Wonder what it means," said Brian.

Norm looked at his middle brother. "What do you mean, you wonder what it means? What does *what* mean? What are you talking about, Brian?"

"I mean, I wonder what your dream means," said Brian. "All dreams mean something."

"No, they don't," said Norm.

"Yeah, they do," said Brian. "I read it in a book."

Norm sighed. "It means nothing. That's what it means."

But even as Norm said it he knew that Brian was probably right. His dream probably *had* meant something. And you didn't need to be a psycho-**flipping-whatever-they-were-called** to figure **what** it meant. It obviously had something to do with moving house and having no money and economising and all that stuff. As for the being naked bit? That was obviously something to do with

Chelsea seeing the photo. The one of him and his best friend, Mikey, without any clothes on. OK, so it had been taken on the beach when they were babies – but even so, it wasn't exactly the sort of thing you wanted to fall

into enemy hands when you were nearly thirteen. Or anytime for that matter. But **especially** when you were nearly thirteen. Which reminded Norm. Chelsea still had the photo. He'd need to do something about that pretty soon.

Norm noticed that Brian was still looking at him.

"What?"

"It means something," said Brian. "It can't just mean nothing."

"It means I got chucked out of a flipping supermarket, that's all!" snapped Norm.

"Language," said Dave.

24

"You can shut up as well, Dave, you little freak!" hissed Norm.

"Now, now, boys," said Norm's mum. "Stop bickering. There's work to do."

Norm pulled a face. "Work?"

"Tidying up your rooms," said Norm's dad.

Of course, thought Norm. His perfect cousins were coming. For some inexplicable reason the house would have to be immaculate. The flipping Queen could be dropping by for afternoon tea and they might vacuum the front room and mop round the toilet but because it was his perfect flipping cousins the whole house was going to have to be cleaned from top to flipping bottom!

"Good job we haven't got the dog yet," said Norm's dad. "There might've been one or two extra things to tidy up."

Brian and Dave laughed.

"I'm serious, boys," said Norm's dad. "This dog had better not make any mess or it'll be straight out."

"That's just reminded me," said Norm.

"What?" said Norm's mum.

"Something else about the dream."

"What?" said Norm's dad.

"Nothing, doesn't matter," said Norm.

"Go on, love," said Norm's mum. "We won't laugh."

"Promise, Mum?"

"Promise."

Norm hesitated. "There was a dog driving a car.

And it could talk."

Brian pulled a face. "The car could talk?"

"Not the car, the **dog**, you doughnut!" said Norm.

"Phew!" said Brian. "Because *that* would've been weird!"

"What? And a talking dog **isn't**?" said Norm.

"Well, you know what they say," said Norm's dad.

"No, Dad," said Norm. "What **do** they say?"

"Friday's dream, Saturday told bound to come true 'ere it ever so old!"

"Uh?" said Dave.

"It's just an expression," said Norm's mum. "It means if you have a dream on a Friday and you tell someone about it the next day it'll come true."

"I flipping hope not," said Norm, deciding it was probably best to keep the bit about being naked in the supermarket to himself.

"Language," said Dave.

CHAPTER 4

As Norm climbed slowly back upstairs he could still make out the faint stains on the carpet where Simon Cowell had done a dump. Stupid name for a dog, thought Norm. Typical Brian though. And typically stupid of Brian to think he could just find a flipping dog and keep it. Which he couldn't. But then his stupid parents only went and promised his brothers a dog to somehow make up for the so-called 'trauma' of having to move house. Unbe-flipping-lievable really, when you thought about it, thought Norm, thinking about it – conveniently forgetting that he hadn't done too badly out of the move himself, getting his bike pimped up.

Norm walked into his bedroom and looked at the posters adorning the walls. One day that would be him on the front of the mountain-biking

magazines. One day that would be him doing a massive jump and posing for the cameras, mid-air. One day that would be him standing on the winner's podium holding the world championship trophy aloft! Not for a few years maybe. It was going to take an awful lot of hard work and dedication between now and then. But he'd get there eventually. His mum and dad somehow scraping together enough money to buy him new front forks, pedals and extra-light handlebars was a step in the right direction.

"Norman?" yelled Norm's mum from the bottom of the stairs.

"Yeah?" yelled Norm.

"I hope you're tidying your room and not just standing there, daydreaming?"

How did she *know*? thought Norm.

30

"Course not, Mum!" yelled Norm.

Norm looked about him. The one good thing about having a room the size of a shoebox was that once he actually got round to tidying it, it didn't take very long. There was no space for a wardrobe or even a chest of drawers. Everything just got stuffed under the bed – including, on one occasion, Dave. No one had even noticed he was missing. It was only when Dave failed to appear for tea that anyone thought to send out a search party. When they eventually found him, he was curled up fast asleep, wedged between a pile of Norm's old pants and a box of Lego Star Wars.

Norm soon got distracted again and before long was flicking through a biking magazine. An article on which particular shape of seat suited which particular shape of bottom proved particularly fascinating.

"Norman?" yelled Norm's mum.

"Yeah?" yelled Norm.

"I hope you've not got distracted?"

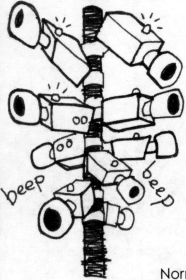

Flipping heck, thought Norm again. How did she *do* that? He was starting to suspect that his mum had rigged up a CCTV camera and was monitoring him from some kind of secret control room deep beneath the house.

"Well?" yelled Norm's mum when Norm failed to answer.

"Well, what, Mum?" yelled Norm, who by now was drooling

32

over an advert for a snazzy new bike app you could get for your smartphone. Not that Norm actually had a smartphone. His flipping phone wasn't even vaguely intelligent, let alone smart, thought Norm bitterly. He could make calls and send texts and that was about it. Frankly, it was embarrassing to be even seen in public with it.

"I said I hope you've not got distracted!" said Norm's mum.

"Course not, Mum!" yelled Norm.

"Good, because they'll be here any minute!"

"Who will?" said Norm.

"Your cousins! Who do you think?" said Norm's mum.

"Aw, flip," muttered Norm under his breath. For a couple of glorious minutes he'd actually forgotten his cousins were coming. Now it was back to earth with a bang.

There was a knock at the front door.

"I'll get it!" yelled Norm's mum, which was just as well since Norm had no intention of getting it himself. The longer he could delay seeing his perfect cousins the better. Every last lingering second counted.

It turned out not to be Norm's cousins at the door after all, but Mikey. It was still lashing down with rain. Mikey could hardly have been wetter if he'd got in the bath fully clothed.

"Oh, it's you, Mikey," said Norm's mum.

"Yeah, it is," grinned Mikey.

There was an awkward silence.

"I would ask you in, Mikey, but I don't want you dripping

water everywhere. We're expecting visitors."

"That's OK," said Mikey.

"No offence."

"None taken."

"Hi, Mikey," said Norm, appearing at his mum's side, having leapt down the stairs three at a time as soon as he'd heard his best friend's voice.

"All right, Norm? You coming out?"

"I'm afraid he can't, Mikey," said Norm's mum before Norm could answer for himself.

"Can't I, Mum?" pleaded Norm.

"You know you can't, love."

"Not even for a few minutes?"

"Not even for a few minutes," said Norm's mum. "Sorry, love."

Norm turned to Mikey, dejected and defeated. Annoyingly the rain had now stopped. As Norm was still showing no signs of being struck down by an incurable tropical disease a walk was looking increasingly inevitable.

"Cousins are coming," he muttered.

"The ones you don't like, you mean?" said Mikey.

"Yeah," said Norm.

"**Norman!**" said Norm's mum.

"Well, I don't," said Norm.

"But they're your cousins!"

"Yeah, so?" said Norm. "Doesn't mean I have

to like them."

"But…"

"You can't **make** me like them, Mum. There's not a law."

"I know, love, but…"

"But what?"

"What is it about them that you don't like?"

"Everything," shot back Norm, like he hadn't even had to think about it. Which he hadn't.

"Everything?" said Norm's mum.

Norm nodded.

"Can you be a bit more specific?"

Norm sighed. "I dunno," he said. "They're just so…"

"So what?" said Norm's mum.

"Just so flipping perfect!"

"What are?" said a voice.

Norm spun round to see a figure standing behind Mikey. Behind the figure were three more figures getting out of a car parked in front of the house.

"Hi, Uncle Steve," said Norm.

"Hi, Norman. Hi, Linda," said Uncle Steve.

"Hello, Steven," said Norm's mum.

"So?" said Uncle Steve. "*What* are so flipping perfect?"

How much had Uncle Steve heard? wondered Norm. Hopefully not *that* much!

"My new handlebars," said Norm, glancing nervously at his mum. Surely it was OK to tell a porky in certain circumstances, wasn't it? And surely this was one of those circumstances?

"Oh, I see," said Uncle Steve. "You still into your bikes then, are you?"

No, I just really like handlebars, thought Norm, making a mental note to himself not to say such stupid things when *he* was as old as Uncle Steve.

"Norman?" said Norm's mum. "Your uncle's talking to you."

"Sorry, what?" said Norm.

"I said, you're still into your bikes then?" said Uncle Steve.

"Yeah," laughed Norm.

"Sorry we're late," said Auntie Jem, appearing at Uncle Steve's side, closely followed by a boy roughly the same age as Norm and a girl a couple of years older.

Not flipping late enough, thought Norm.

"Danny's just been swimming and Becky had a rehearsal," said Auntie Jem, without waiting to be asked.

"Hello, Linda, by the way," said Auntie Jem. "Hello, Norman. I expect you're too old for a hug, are you?"

"I expect I am," said Norm quickly.

"So, you've been swimming, have you, Danny?" said Norm's mum. "What a shame, Norman. You could have gone too if you'd known."

"Actually, no, he couldn't," said Auntie Jem. "It was a competition. Wasn't it, Danny?"

Danny nodded sheepishly.

"I see!" said Norm's mum. "And how did you get on, Danny?"

"He won, didn't you, Danny?" said Auntie Jem.

Danny nodded again.

"Well done," said Norm's mum. "What stroke, Danny?"

"All of them," said Auntie Jem.

"Congratulations," said Norm's mum.

This had to be some sort of record, thought Norm. His flipping cousins weren't even in the door and already he wanted to puke.

"And what are you rehearsing, Becky?" said Norm's mum.

"*Hamlet*," said Auntie Jem.

"Really? What part?" said Norm's mum.

All of them? thought Norm.

"Oh, she's not actually in it," said Auntie Jem. "She's directing. Aren't you, Becky?"

Becky smiled sweetly.

"Wow!" said Norm's mum. "That's very impressive, Becky."

"It's not that big a deal," said Uncle Steve modestly.

Auntie Jem glared venomously at her husband, leaving no one in any doubt that in her opinion, a fifteen-year-old girl directing Shakespeare wasn't just a *big* deal, it was a *massive* deal.

"And where's Ed?" said Norm's mum.

"Oh, he's away with the Scouts," said Uncle Steve.

"Climbing Mount Kilimanjaro," added Auntie Jem.

Course he is, thought Norm. He couldn't just be camping in some flipping farmer's field half an hour away where his parents could come and get him if he got too cold, could he? He had to be climbing up Mount Kiliman-flipping-jaro! Wherever **that** was!

"It's in Tanzania," said Danny quietly to Norm.

"I knew that," said Norm, who not only **didn't** know that, but also suspected that Tanzania wasn't even a proper country.

"I'd better be off then," said Mikey, turning to leave.

"Good idea, Mikey," said Norm's mum. "Get out of those wet things before you catch cold."

"Mikey?" said Uncle Steve.

"Yeah," said Mikey, stopping.

"Goodness me, I hardly recognised you!"

You **didn't**, thought Norm.

"It must be what? Three or four years?"

Since **what**? thought Norm.

"Well, *you've* certainly grown!" said Uncle Steve.

Be pretty flipping weird if he *hadn't*, thought Norm, getting increasingly exasperated.

Mikey shuffled around as if he didn't know quite what to say. Norm knew **exactly** what *he'd* like to say but decided it was probably best not to.

"Well, don't let us stop you," said Uncle Steve.

"'Kay, bye," said Mikey, setting off down the path again.

"Yeah, bye," said Norm, following Mikey outside.

"Norman?" said Norm's mum, raising her eyebrows.

"Yeah?" said Norm innocently.

"We're going for a walk, remember?"

"Oh, yeah," said Norm. "Forgot. Silly me."

CHAPTER 5

"So what have *you* been up to lately, Norman?" said Uncle Steve, pleasantly.

An expectant hush descended around the table. Clanking of cutlery ceased. Heads turned towards Norm.

"Norman!" said Norm's mum. "What have I told you about listening to your iPod while we're eating?"

There was no reply from Norm. Norm's mum nudged him with her elbow.

"  "   "Sorry, what, Mum?"
said Norm, taking his headphones off.

"Uncle Steve's trying to talk to you! So rude!"

"I dunno, kids today," said Dave. "No respect for their elders."

"Sorry, Uncle Steve," said Norm. "What were you saying?"

"I was just wondering what you've been up to lately, that's all," said Uncle Steve, smiling. "Apart from riding your bike."

Norm thought for a moment. It was a good question. What *had* he been up to lately apart from riding his bike?

"Not much," said Norm.

"How's school?"

"It's all right, I suppose."

"Got a girlfriend?"

"  "   shrieked Norm.

"Why not?" grinned Uncle Steve.

Why not? thought Norm. Because getting a girlfriend was even further down his list of priorities than tidying his room, *that's* why not! Not that Norm actually *had* a list of priorities. But if he did have one, getting a girlfriend would be way down it and probably not even on it at all. And anyway, what *was* this? A meal, or a flipping quiz?

"Come on, Steve," said Norm's mum. "He's only twelve!"

"Nearly thirteen actually," muttered Norm.

"Sorry, Norman," said Uncle Steve. "I was only teasing you."

"Why have you gone red, Norman?" said Brian.

"I haven't gone red!" snapped Norm, knowing perfectly well that he had.

"Yeah, you have!" said Brian.

"Anyway, he *has* got a girlfriend," said Dave. "Her name's Chelsea."

"Shut up, Dave!" said Norm. "Chelsea is *not* my girlfriend!"

Danny sniggered. "Don't tell me," he said. "She's a friend who just *happens* to be a girl."

"She's not a girl!" said Norm.

"What?" said Brian.

"I mean she's not a friend," said Norm. "Look, I have **not** got a flipping girlfriend, all right?"

"The lady doth protest too much, methinks," said Becky.

48

"*Hamlet*," beamed Auntie Jem.

"Act three, scene two," said Becky.

Whatever, thought Norm.

"She must like *you*, Norman," said Brian. "She's got a photo of you."

"Shut up, Brian!" said Norm.

"The one of you with no..."

"**I'm warning you, Brian!**" hissed Norm.

"Dessert, anyone?" said Norm's dad, getting up and heading for the kitchen.

Norm was still working his way through the main course. And he *still* had no idea what it was. Noodles and crunchy green things and some spongy stuff that looked and felt like marshmallow but which tasted like loft insulation. Not that Norm had ever actually tasted loft insulation. But he imagined that's what it would taste like if he did.

"What's this, Mum?" said Norm, holding up a piece of the spongy stuff on the end of his fork.

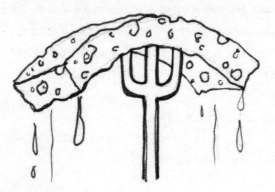

"Tofu!" said Norm's mum.

"What?" said Norm.

"Bean curd," said Becky. "Made from soy milk. Very nutritious."

"You know that, love!" laughed Norm's mum. "We have it all the time!"

No, we don't, thought Norm. And why was his mum talking in that funny voice?

"It was very nice, Linda," said Auntie Jem. "I particularly liked the way the vegetables were slightly undercooked."

Norm looked at Auntie Jem, unsure whether this was supposed to be a compliment or an insult.

"Really?" said Norm's mum, apparently not too sure herself.

"Really," said Auntie Jem. "You could taste the goodness!"

If *that's* what goodness tasted like, you could flipping keep it, thought Norm, whose idea of a balanced diet was a pizza in each hand.

"Wow!" said Uncle Steve as Norm's dad came back carrying a tray. "Someone's been busy!"

"Oh, it's nothing really," said Norm's dad, putting the tray down on the table. "Just something I whipped up."

"What is it?" said Uncle Steve. "It looks amazing!"

"Cinnamon-infused dates with meringue topping, drizzled with raspberry coulis," said Norm's dad matter-of-factly.

What-infused *what* with *what*, drizzled with *what*? thought Norm. Had the whole world gone flipping mad?

"Mmmm, delicious," said Uncle Steve, tucking in. "You must give me the recipe, Alan."

Great idea, thought Norm. Then his dad wouldn't be able to make it again. They could go back to eating proper food instead of all this weird stuff.

"Were the eggs free-range, Uncle Alan?" asked Becky.

"Pardon?" said Norm's dad.

"The eggs you used to make the meringue topping?" said Becky. "Were they free-range?"

"Becky can't eat eggs laid by battery hens," explained Auntie Jem.

Can't, or won't? thought Norm.

"Oh, free-range, of course," said Norm's mum. "We wouldn't buy any other kind. Terribly cruel, cooping those poor creatures up like that."

Norm's mum shot Norm a quick warning glance, daring him to say something to the contrary.

Norm – who knew perfectly well that the eggs would have been the cheapest in the supermarket, laid by the scrawniest hens packed together tighter than commuters on a rush-hour train – **thought** about saying something, but decided not to.

He was quite looking forward to seeing what might happen if Becky literally **couldn't** eat battery-laid eggs. With any luck she might projectile vomit all over the table and the walk would get cancelled. Norm chuckled at the thought.

"What is it, love?" said Norm's mum.

"Nothing," said Norm.

CHAPTER 6

Unfortunately as far as Norm was concerned, there was no projectile vomiting at the table and the walk with the perfect cousins wasn't cancelled. On the plus side though, thought Norm – lagging so far behind the others he was practically in a different postcode – just because you were forced to **walk** with someone didn't mean you were forced to *talk* with them.

What would they find to talk **about** anyway? As far as Norm could see, he and his cousins had absolutely nothing in common, other than the fact that his cousins were also human and frankly even then, Norm had his doubts. He wouldn't have been in the least bit surprised to discover they hadn't actually been born, but created by scientists in some kind of secret laboratory. Surely they must have *some* faults, mustn't they? Something they weren't brilliant at? Some kind of weakness? Even superheroes had weaknesses.

They were walking by the river. Well, strictly speaking everyone *else* was walking by the river. Norm was **trudging** by the river. Any slower and he'd have been going backwards. It had started to rain again. Everything was grey and bleak and miserable. Even the ducks looked fed up. Ahead, Norm could see Brian and Dave chatting and laughing alongside Becky. Flipping creeps, thought Norm.

Someone shot past on a bike. Norm watched enviously as they quickly disappeared into the distance. What *he* wouldn't give to be on *his* bike right now. Jumping the steps at the back of the precinct. Whizzing down the trail through the woods. Launching himself off a ramp on Mikey's drive.

The next thing he knew, Norm was standing on the winner's podium, his adoring fans chanting his name as once again he was proclaimed World Mountain Biking Champion.

The next thing he knew after *that*, Norm was standing in front of a house. Not just any old house. His old house.

Norm couldn't believe it. What the heck were his parents thinking? How can we make Norm even **more** angry? How can we make him think that life's even *more* unfair? How can we make him resent us even **more**? Because if they were, thought Norm, they were going about it in the right way. Of all the stupid, insensitive things they could have done, this took the flipping biscuit! In fact, never mind *one* flipping biscuit! This took a whole packet of flipping biscuits! And not just rich teas, or digestives either! Jammie flipping Dodgers!

"Ever wish you still lived here?" said Danny, appearing at Norm's side.

"No," blurted Norm. "Why would I?"

"Dunno," said Danny. "Because it's bigger?"

Danny was right. Norm's old house *was* bigger than the one they lived in now. Not *massively* bigger. And not as big as his perfect cousins' house of course. But it was bigger all the same. Danny knew that. Norm knew that. Danny knew that Norm knew that. Norm knew that Danny knew that Norm knew that.

"Is it?" said Norm casually. "Can't say I've noticed."

"Really?" said Danny doubtfully.

"Yeah, really," said Norm, wishing that Danny would clear off and leave him in peace again. If they'd still been by the river Norm would have been tempted to push him in. See how good he *really* was at swimming.

Danny got his phone out and pointed it at the house.

"What are you doing?" said Norm.

"Taking a picture," said Danny.

"You can't do that!"

"Just did," said Danny. "Wanna look?"

"Not particularly," said Norm.

It was true. Norm *didn't* particularly want a look. What was the point? They were standing right in front of the house. What did he want to see a flipping picture of it for? It would be like texting someone standing next to you. But it was too late. Danny had already shoved his phone in front of Norm's face.

"Great," said Norm, who couldn't help noticing that it was a dead expensive

phone. The sort of phone

that Norm could only dream of owning. And that was one dream that was never ever going to come true, whether Norm told someone about it on a Saturday or any other flipping day for that matter. "The picture, I mean," added Norm quickly. "Not the phone."

But it was too late. Danny had detected a faint whiff of jealousy. "Not bad, eh?"

Norm shrugged. "It's all right, I suppose. If you like that kind of thing."

Danny smiled. "Why? Don't you then?"

"Don't I what?"

"Like that kind of thing?"

"Phones, you mean?" said Norm.

"Yeah," said Danny.

Norm thought for a second. What should he say? Of course he liked phones. What nearly thirteen-year-old kid in their right mind **didn't** like phones? But the last thing he wanted was to give Danny the satisfaction of knowing that he was impressed by *his* flipping phone. Even though he **was** impressed. He was well impressed.

"They're OK, I suppose," said Norm, nonchalantly.

"What have you got?"

"What kind of **phone** have I got?" said Norm, deliberately stalling for time and knowing perfectly well that that was what Danny had meant.

"Yeah," said Danny.

"Oh, nothing fancy," said Norm.

Danny grinned, clearly relishing the situation. "Can I see it?"

"What?" said Norm. "Nah, haven't got it on me."

"Really?"

Norm nodded. "Needed charging."

"Right," said Danny.

They looked at each other for a moment. It had stopped raining. Everything had gone very quiet and still. So when a phone suddenly started ringing from somewhere inside Norm's trousers, it somehow seemed even louder and more shrill than it would have done otherwise.

"Oops, my mistake," said Norm, delving into a pocket. "I *have* got it on me. Silly me."

Norm got his phone out and answered it, at the same time doing his best to shield it from

Danny's gaze.

"Hi, Dad."

Norm listened for a moment.

"Yeah, yeah, we're just coming."

Norm listened some more.

"'Kay, Dad. Bye, Dad."

Norm ended the call and pocketed his phone again. But the damage had already been done. His perfect cousin, Danny, had seen it. It was official. Norm had the world's oldest, most out-of-date, most rubbish phone.

"Go on then," said Norm, setting off down the road.

"What do you mean?" said Danny, following.

"Get it over with."

"Get *what* over with?" said Danny.

"Take the mickey," said Norm.

Danny pulled a face. "It's not *that* bad!"

Norm pulled a face back.

"**Are you SERIOUS?!** it's over a year old."

Danny laughed.

"Honestly!" said Norm. "I've seen **newer** phones on *The Antiques Road Show!*"

Norm wasn't kidding. He was genuinely mortified at being caught red-handed with such an embarrassingly ancient phone. He'd been hoping to get a new one for his birthday but then his stupid dad just had to go and get himself flipping sacked, didn't he? Now they were skint. There was more chance of Norm taking up ballet than there was of him getting a new phone. And there was no chance of that. It was *so* unfair.

Norm noticed Danny was looking at him. "What?"

Danny hesitated. "You probably think I just got given this phone for no reason whatsoever, don't you?"

Bullseye, thought Norm. That was *exactly* what he thought.

"You probably think we're spoilt, don't you?"

Bullseye again, thought Norm. It was almost like Danny could read his mind.

"Well?" said Danny. "You do, don't you?"

"Dunno," shrugged Norm. "Maybe."

"I didn't just get *given* it," said Danny. "I had to *earn* it."

Earn it? thought Norm. How? Not by tidying his flipping room for a start. He probably had servants to do that for him.

They walked on in silence. The others were way out of sight by now.

"Aren't you going to ask me how?" said Danny eventually.

"How what?" said Norm.

"How I earned the phone?"

"Erm. Wasn't going to, no," said Norm.

Norm looked across at his cousin. There was something a little different about him. But what? Norm couldn't quite put his finger on it. He wasn't even sure he *wanted* to put his finger on it. All Norm wanted was for Danny to shut up and walk. The quicker they got back, the quicker he'd be out on his bike.

"I got it for getting a good report," said Danny.

That figured, thought Norm.

"A *very* good report," said Danny.

All right, all right, thought Norm. He got the picture. No need to rub it in.

Danny hesitated slightly. "A bit *too* good, as a matter of fact."

Norm sighed. He was actually becoming just a teensy bit intrigued and he hated himself for it. "What are you on about? What do you mean a bit **too** good?"

Danny looked at Norm. "Can you keep a secret?"

"Depends," said Norm.

"I faked it," blurted Danny, without bothering to find out what it depended on.

Norm stopped. Had he heard right?

"You *what?*" said Norm.

"I faked it," said Danny. "I faked my own report!"

"Yeah, right," laughed Norm.

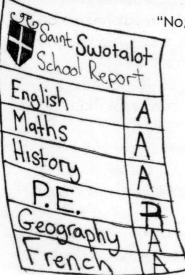

Saint Swotalot
School Report

English	A
Maths	A
History	A
P.E.	A
Geography	A
French	A

"No, really, I did," insisted Danny.

"How?"

"Changed a 'B' to an 'A'."

"Just one?"

Danny nodded. "I got 'A's for everything else anyway."

Course he did, thought Norm. Silly question. But still. Danny – his perfect cousin, Danny – had **faked** his report! This was gobsmacking news of the very highest gobsmacking order. It was like finding out your parents still snogged each other – though admittedly not quite as gross.

"Whoa," said Norm.

Danny suddenly looked relieved. Like he'd had something stuck in his throat and someone had just given him a good whack on the back.

"I had to tell someone. It was driving me mad."

"Whoa," said Norm again.

"Not quite so perfect now, am I?"

Norm pulled a face. "How did you know that's what I called you?"

"I didn't," smiled Danny. "But I do now."

"It's nothing personal," said Norm.

"It's OK," said Danny. "It could be worse I suppose."

"So that was the deal, was it?" said Norm. "A new phone if you got straight 'A's?"

Danny never got the chance to answer. At that moment his phone rang. He looked to see who it was.

"Sorry, I've really got to take this."

And I've *really* got to have one of those, thought Norm as Danny answered his dead expensive, bang-up-to-date phone.

"Hi, Mum," said Danny.

There was just one teensy problem, thought Norm. He had no money. And as far as he knew, neither did his mum or dad.

"'Kay, Mum," said Danny. "I'll see you in a minute. Bye, Mum."

Danny ended the call and set off down the road at a brisk trot.

"Gotta go!" he called.
"Capoeira!"

Norm had no idea what Danny was talking about, or indeed what language he was talking about it in. But at that moment Norm couldn't have cared less. He'd just discovered that his so-called perfect cousin had a weakness. He'd faked his own school report. He might just be human after all!

Norm smiled to himself. You just never knew when this kind of information might come in useful.

CHAPTER 7

By the time Norm eventually got home, his perfect cousin, Becky, and his not-quite-so perfect cousin, Danny, had already left.

"Oh dear, what a pity," muttered Norm sarcastically to no one in particular.

Norm's mood improved even more when he walked into the kitchen and saw his mum getting a bag of chips and some sausages out of the freezer. Thank goodness for that, he thought. Normal stuff for tea. No more spongy loft insulation. No more crunchy green things. He could just imagine the look on Becky's face. Are the sausages free-range, Uncle Alan? Are the chips fair trade, Uncle Alan? Were the potatoes humanely peeled, Uncle Alan? But Becky wasn't there, was she? There was no longer any need to impress Auntie Jem. They could all just flipping well relax.

"Well?" said Norm's mum.

"Well, what?" said Norm.

"That wasn't too bad, was it?"

Norm considered this for a moment. On reflection the walk **hadn't** been **quite** as bad as he'd expected. But then it was all relative, wasn't it? He'd convinced himself it was going to be pant-soilingly horrific. So anything **less** than pant-soilingly horrific was going to be a bonus. And in light of certain revelations – or a certain revelation anyway – it could even turn out to have been a very **useful** walk. Norm hadn't got round to working out exactly **how** it might be useful. Not yet. But he would sooner or later. Preferably sooner.

"Well?" said Norm's mum. "Was it?"

"It was all right, I suppose," said Norm with as much enthusiasm as he could muster. Which wasn't much.

"Good," said Norm's mum. "Because we've arranged to visit *them* next weekend."

"What?" said Norm.

"We're going to your cousins' next weekend."

Norm's good mood evaporated in an instant, like a bubble rising to the surface in a glass of lemonade. One second it was there – and the next? **Pffff!** It was gone.

"But we've seen them once already this year," said Norm. "What do we need to see them again for?"

"To walk the dog," said Norm's mum.

Norm looked puzzled. "But we don't have a dog, Mum."

"No, but we should have by next weekend."

"What?" said Norm.

"There was a message from the dogs' home on the answering machine," explained Norm's mum.

Norm had forgotten. Someone had been to check the house out and make sure it was big enough for a dog to live in. They were having a laugh, thought Norm bitterly. It was scarcely big enough for a flipping human to live in, let alone a flipping dog!

EEK!

"They said everything's fine," said Norm's mum.

"Unbelievable," muttered Norm.

"We're getting a dog! We're getting a dog!" sang Brian and Dave, suddenly bursting into the kitchen.

"Well, *hopefully* we are, boys," said Norm's mum. "We'll go and see what they've got."

Norm pulled a face. "Why don't you just get one online?"

"You're not serious, are you, love?"

Norm shrugged. "Be much easier."

"You can't just buy a dog on the internet."

"Why not?" said Norm. It seemed perfectly reasonable. You could get just about anything you could think of on the internet.

"It's obvious," said Dave. "You'd never get it through the letter box!"

Brian regarded his little brother with barely concealed disdain. "Don't be so stupid, Dave."

"Mum!" whined Dave. "Brian said I'm stupid!"

"What's your point?" said Norm.

"Now, now, that's enough," said Norm's mum. "Why don't you go out in the garden and play nicely together?"

Play **nicely** together? thought Norm. With his brothers? How old did his mum think he was? Three or something? And *what* flipping garden was that, by the way? Norm had seen bigger postage stamps!

"Go on," said Norm's mum. "Leave me in peace. I'm trying to cook here."

Norm watched his mum as she opened the bag of frozen chips and spread them out on a baking tray. Now *that* was his kind of cooking! Sausage and chips? **Drizzled** with ketchup? Norm couldn't flipping wait!

CHAPTER 8

Norm chose not to play with his brothers. Not only did he like to think that he actually **had** a life, he wanted to look at phones on the internet instead. It was funny, thought Norm, sitting down in front of the computer. If he'd had a better phone he would have been able to look at phones on his phone. But then, if he'd had a better phone, he probably wouldn't have been looking at phones. He'd have been looking at something completely different.

Norm sighed.

Why did life have to be so flipping complicated sometimes?

It didn't take long to find Danny's phone. Norm whistled. He knew it was expensive, but he had no idea it was *that* expensive! He was obviously wasting his time. He was never ever going to have enough money to get one.

Unless...

unless...

unless...

Unless what? thought Norm. Unless he won the lottery? He wasn't old enough to *do* the lottery, let alone flipping win it. Unless he discovered a suitcase of money in an old tumbledown house somewhere? What

was this? A flipping movie or something? Unless he offered to do the washing up every day till he was thirty? Yeah – like *that* was going to happen.

It was *so* unfair, thought Norm, gazing out of the window. Just when he needed an *unless* the most, he couldn't flipping think of one.

Outside in the garden, Dave was squatting on the grass, pretending to do a dump. Brian was busy pretending to pick up whatever Dave had pretended to do, with a plastic bag. At least that's what Norm thought his brothers were doing. He never had been any good at mime – either doing it himself, or guessing what other people were doing. Mime was a bit like going for a walk as far as Norm was concerned. He just couldn't see the point.

So they were getting this stupid dog tomorrow, were they? Very soon Brian and Dave would be picking up **real** mounds of steaming canine poo from the lawn. And it *would* be Brian and Dave too, thought Norm, because there was no flipping way *he* was ever doing it – and if his mum and dad thought he was, they had another flipping thing coming!

Suddenly the computer beeped. Mikey was online and wanting to chat. Norm opened up the box and typed.

hi

hi
replied Mikey a moment later.

wot?
typed Norm.

gess hoo a frend of a frend of a frend of mine is on facebook

Norm had no idea who a friend of a friend of a friend of Mikey's was on Facebook. If indeed that's what the question was. Mikey's spelling and complete lack of punctuation was even worse than Norm's. And that was saying something.

who?
typed Norm.

chelsea
replied Mikey.

so?
typed Norm.

the gurl not the football team

obviously
typed Norm.

she sent me a message

who did?

chelsea

and?

2 wurds

HURRY UP AND FLIPPING TELL ME THEM
MIKEY YOU DONUT
typed Norm, furiously.

Mikey's reply popped up almost immediately.

baby foto

Norm stared at the screen. It was pretty much all he **could** do since he'd temporarily lost the ability to type. Alarm bells were going off in his head. He should have guessed. Or rather, **gessed**. The photo. The one of him and Mikey. The one of him and Mikey **naked**. Naked with no clothes on. In the buff. No packets of coco pops to cover their modesty. Well – Norm's modesty. You couldn't see Mikey's modesty. He had his back to the camera.

she saying shes going 2 post it? typed Norm, now seriously beginning to panic.

Norm clicked send and waited. He felt as sick as the sickest parrot in a sick parrot hospital. The thought of him and his dangly bits being up there on Facebook for all to see was too much to bear. It made no difference to Norm that they were only baby dangly bits. They were **his** flipping dangly bits and he didn't want anyone else looking at them thank you very much! He'd be a laughing stock. People would point at him in the street. He'd never hear the last of it!

There was a beep from the computer. Mikey had replied.

not going 2

Norm breathed an enormous sigh of relief. But Mikey hadn't finished.

alredy has

Relief quickly turned to disbelief. Disbelief turned to shock. Shock turned to dread and finally, dread turned to Norm wanting to punch something very hard indeed. She'd already done it. She'd already flipping well gone and done it! What kind of sick and twisted mind would do something like that? thought Norm. Even *he* wouldn't do something like **that**. Probably.

Norm looked out of the window. Brian was repeatedly throwing a stick for his younger brother to fetch. Time after time Dave bounded after the stick on all fours and each time he brought it back he'd roll over and let Brian tickle his tummy. Norm shook his head. What was wrong with them? They should be inside, on the Xbox or watching television – not playing flipping dogs!

But then it suddenly occurred to Norm. It wasn't Chelsea he should really be angry at. OK, so she'd actually posted the photo on Facebook. But it was **Brian** who'd given her the photo in the first place. It was Brian who would have to pay for it one way or another. It was **Brian** who would feel the full wrath of Norm. It was **Brian** who was going to have to face the consequences sooner or later.

Preferably sooner.

CHAPTER 9

Norm sat wedged in the back of the car, his face pressed up against the window. And he wasn't happy. Why did **he** have to go to the flipping dogs' home? It was stupid o'clock on a Sunday morning! He had things to do! Like sleep!

His brothers' incessant jabbering and gibbering was doing nothing to improve Norm's already foul mood. He could barely make out a word they were saying. All he could hear was a high-pitched monotonous drone. It was like sitting next to a pair of wasps.

Norm tried turning his iPod up. But it was no good. He could still hear Brian and Dave. Dog this, dog that, dog the other. He tried pulling his hood over his head and around his face. But that was no good either. He could **still** hear them.

"*Are we there yet?*"

said Dave.

"Does it *look* like we're there yet?" snapped Norm from somewhere deep within his hood.

"No," said Dave.

"Can you see any signs saying *Dogs' Home*?"

"No," said Dave.

"Well then," said Norm. "We're not there yet, Dave, you doughnut!"

"Now, now, love," said Norm's mum. "No need to be like that."

"Like what?" said Norm.

"*That!*" said Norm's dad.

Norm sighed.

"And you can pack *that* in!" said Norm's dad.

"What?" said Norm. "***I didn't do anything!***"

"You sighed," said Norm's dad.

This was getting ridiculous, thought Norm. Not only had he been dragged out his bed in the middle of the night to go and look for a flipping dog, he couldn't even sigh now.

They drove on in silence for a while.

"I saw a lovely kennel on one of the shopping channels," said Norm's mum eventually.

"Cool," said Brian.

"Hmm, yes," said Norm's mum. "Like a miniature house."

Norm couldn't believe what he was hearing. A miniature house? What did they want a miniature house for? They had one already. The one they flipping lived in! If they put another one in the garden it would look like an extension!

"Why don't we wait to see what kind of dog we get first?" said Norm's dad. "We might not actually *need* a kennel."

This conversation was getting weirder and weirder, thought Norm, imagining rows and rows of dogs arranged according to size like some kind of pet supermarket. Which reminded Norm. The dream.

The one where he was standing at a checkout naked. Which reminded Norm. The naked baby photo. Which reminded Norm. It was all Brian's fault.

Norm peeped through the slit in his hood and groaned. They were passing his school.

"Something wrong, love?" said Norm's mum.

"What?" said Norm distractedly.

"You groaned," said Norm's dad.

So groaning's not allowed now either, thought Norm. He really must make a note of these things for future reference.

"Are you feeling OK?" said Norm's mum.

"Not really," said Norm. Which was true. He **wasn't** feeling OK. In fact he was feeling anything **but** OK. Tomorrow could well turn out to be the most humiliating day of his life so far. **Everyone** would have seen the naked baby photo by then. Never mind sticking it up on Facebook. They might as well stick it up on a giant billboard in the middle of the flipping town!

"You're not going to throw up, are you?" said Brian.

"If I am I'll make sure it's over you," hissed Norm.

"Why? What have I done?" asked Brian innocently.

What have you *done*? thought Norm. Where did he start? "You mean you don't know, Brian?"

"I don't know what you're talking about," said Brian.

Norm smiled. Brian really *didn't* know what he'd done. He'd simply given the photo to Chelsea and thought that was that. Well, that *wasn't* that, thought Norm. There were going to be consequences. For both Norm *and* Brian. Revenge – no matter how long it took – was somehow going to taste all the sweeter.

"I can see one!" said Dave excitedly.

"One what?" said Norm.

"A sign!" said Dave.

"What?" said Norm.

"A sign saying *Dogs' Home*!"

"Yeah!" shrieked Brian. "We're there!"

The car slowed to a halt.

"Right, you lot," said Norm's dad, switching off the engine. "Everybody out."

Brian and Dave were off like a shot. Norm, meanwhile, showed no signs of moving.

"Norman?" said Norm's dad.

"Yeah?" said Norm.

"That includes you."

Norm pulled a face.

"And you can pack *that* in as well!" said Norm's dad.

"Pack what in?" said Norm.

"Pulling faces!"

Norm was confused. "How did you know, Dad? I've got my hood pulled over my face."

Norm's dad chuckled. "So I was right then," he said.

Norm had fallen for it. He could have kicked himself, except that probably wasn't allowed. And he couldn't pull faces now. He'd add it to the flipping list.

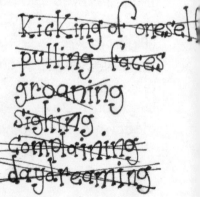

Kicking of oneself
pulling faces
groaning
sighing
complaining
daydreaming

CHAPTER 10

Approaching the dogs' home, decided Norm, was a bit like approaching his brothers. It was the noise that hit you first – and **then** the smell. The one major difference between Brian and Dave and the dogs' home, as far as Norm could see, was that Brian and Dave weren't surrounded by a high brick wall topped with barbed wire. Whether that was to stop the dogs getting out, or to stop people getting in and nicking the dogs, Norm wasn't quite sure.

"I still don't see why I had to come," said Norm, trying to make himself heard above the din.

"Sorry, love," said Norm's mum. "You'll have to speak up!"

"I said I still don't see why I had to come!" said Norm, a bit louder. "There's no point! It's not me getting a dog – it's Brian and Dave! If I was getting a new phone I wouldn't expect **them** to come and look at it!"

Not that *that* was likely to happen in the near future, thought Norm. Or the future full-flipping-stop come to think of it.

"Sorry, love," said Norm's mum. "Didn't catch a word of that!"

"Pardon?" said Norm.

"I said I didn't catch a word of that!" yelled Norm's mum. "What did you say?"

"Doesn't matter," muttered Norm.

"Pardon?" yelled Norm's mum.

"Doesn't matter!" yelled Norm.

"No need to shout!" yelled Norm's mum.

Yeah, there is, thought Norm. By now the racket really was unbe-flipping-lievable! Even worse than some of the so-called 'music' his parents listened to. And **that** was flipping saying something. You couldn't hear the words. There wasn't even a proper beat. It was what Norm imagined the end of the world would sound like – except louder. But then if *he* turned **his** music up even a fraction above normal conversational level he got told to turn it down again! It was *so* flipping unfair!

"Hi, guys!" said a very smiley woman, as Norm reluctantly followed his mum and the others into the reception area. "What can I do for you today?"

You can stop being so flipping cheerful for a start, thought Norm.

"We'd like a dog, please," said Brian.

"Well, you've certainly come to the right place!" laughed the woman.

"We had someone come round," said Norm's mum. "They said that everything's fine."

"Unfortunately," muttered Norm.

"Norman?" said Norm's dad sternly.

"Any particular kind of dog in mind?" said the smiley dogs' home woman.

"What have you got?" said Dave.

"Ooh, we've got all sorts," said the woman.

"Erm, in that case I'd like a brown one please," said Dave.

Norm glared at his little brother. What did he think he was doing? Choosing a dog or a flipping flavour of ice cream?

"A brown one, eh?" smiled the woman.

"Yes, please," said Dave.

"Or a black one," said Brian. "Or a white one. Or one with lots of different colours. It doesn't matter really."

"Do you want a flake with it?" said Norm.

"A flake?" said Brian. "What are you on about, Norman?"

"Doesn't matter," said Norm.

"We don't really mind what colour it is as long as it's fully house-trained," said Norm's dad.

House-trained? thought Norm. What – one that tidied up and could load the dishwasher? Perhaps getting a dog wasn't *such* a bad idea after all.

"We can't guarantee there won't be the odd little accident," said the woman. "A lot of these dogs have led very traumatic lives."

Tell me about it, thought Norm.

"Some of them have been deprived of any kind of warmth, or love, or human affection."

Welcome to my world, thought Norm.

"They're mentally scarred."

Yeah, so? thought Norm. Who isn't? That's no excuse for running around, dumping on the carpet – otherwise *he'd* be doing it all the flipping time!

"Let's go and have a look, shall we?" said the woman, leading the way through a door and out into the open.

The noise, which had been relatively muffled inside the reception area, suddenly got incredibly loud again as each and every dog began barking its head off and generally going bonkers. As for the smell? Norm had never experienced anything so disgusting in all his life. It was like some kind of evil combination of blocked school toilets on a hot summer's day and something that had crawled behind a radiator and died. Norm tried holding his nose and breathing through his mouth. But it was no good. He could **still** smell it.

"What's up?" said Brian.

"Can you not smell it?" said Norm.

"Smell what?" said Brian. "I can't smell a thing. Can you, Dave?"

Dave sniffed. "Nah."

Norm stared at his brothers in disbelief. "Just hurry up and flipping choose one!"

"How about this guy?" said the woman, standing in front of an enclosure. Behind a wire-mesh fence was a small dog with droopy ears and a coat of tight golden curls. "It's called a cock-a-poo."

Norm pulled a face. Had he heard right?

"A what-a-poo?"

"A cock-a-poo," repeated the woman. "A cross between a cocker spaniel and a poodle. A cock-a-poo."

Norm burst out laughing. He **had** heard right!

"What's so funny about that?" said Norm's dad.

"What's **not** funny about it?" said Norm.

Norm's dad shook his head in exasperation. "How old are you, Norman?"

"Nearly thirteen," said Norm. Brilliant. So his own father didn't even know how old he was.

"Then act like it," said Norm's dad.

"Yeah, Norman," said Dave. "You're so immature!"

"Shut up, Dave, you little freak!" spat Norm.

The dog, meanwhile, had rolled onto its back and was whimpering softly.

"He's so cute!" said Brian.

"How do you know it's a he?" said Dave.

"Look," said Brian, pointing.

Dave looked.
"Oh yeah."

Norm giggled.

"I'm warning you!" said Norm's dad, which somehow only made Norm want to giggle even more.

"What's his name?" said Brian.

"We call him Lucky," said the smiley dogs' home woman.

"Why?" said Brian.

"He was found abandoned by the side of a motorway," said the woman. "It was a miracle he didn't get run over."

"Ah, that's so sad," said Dave.

"You should call him Willy," spluttered Norm, by now barely able to control himself.

"Right! That's it!" shouted Norm's dad. "Get back to the car, Norman! And stay there!"

No problem, thought Norm, catching the car key his dad had just lobbed in his direction. No problem at all!

CHAPTER 11

Norm made a beeline for his bike the moment they got back from the dogs' home. Lunch could wait. Norm needed time out. And what better way of spending that time than practising wheelies on the drive?

"What are you doing, **Norman?**" said a voice from over the fence two seconds later.

Norm gritted his teeth. Why did Chelsea always put on a weird voice and overemphasise his name like that? Did she think she was being funny? Because if she did she was wrong. It wasn't funny the first time and it wasn't funny the **hundred** and flipping first time. At least it was a *proper* name. At least he wasn't named after a flipping football team!

"I want a word with you," said Norm, ignoring Chelsea's question.

"I'm feeling generous," said Chelsea. "Have two."

"You put that photo up on Facebook."

"What photo," said Chelsea, knowing perfectly well what photo Norm meant.

Norm pulled a face, knowing perfectly well that Chelsea knew perfectly well what photo he meant.

"Oh, *that* photo! Yeah, so?"

"You said you wouldn't if I let you keep that twenty pounds."

"Did I?" said Chelsea. "Oops."

"Oops?" said Norm. "Is that all you've got to say? **Oops?**"

Chelsea shrugged. Apparently it *was* all she'd got to say.

"Why?" said Norm.

"*Why* is that all I've got to say? said Chelsea.

"Why did you do it?" said Norm.

"It's funny," said Chelsea.

"You call that funny?" said Norm. "Posting a photo of someone naked on Facebook? I've got to go to school tomorrow!"

"Yeah? So? So have I," said Chelsea.

Norm sighed. There was no point arguing. Chelsea seemed to have an answer for everything. Somehow it was different with his little brothers. He could boss them around. He was the one in charge.

But there was just something about Chelsea that... that... Norm wasn't sure what it was about Chelsea. All he knew was that whenever he planned to confront her, or challenge her about something, things always seemed to go pear-shaped.

"Anyway, I don't see what the big deal is," said Chelsea. "You can't see much."

Norm had a feeling there was a punchline coming. And he was right.

"There wasn't much to see," laughed Chelsea.

Norm immediately felt himself blushing.

"What's the matter?" said Chelsea.

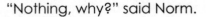

"Nothing, why?" said Norm.

"You've gone bright red."

"No, I haven't," said Norm. But he knew he had.

"So?"

"So, what?" said Norm.

"What are you going to do about it?" said Chelsea.

It was a good point, thought Norm. What *was* he going to do about it?

"Make you take it down?" said Norm, not terribly convincingly.

"Oh, yeah?" said Chelsea. "And why should I do that then?"

"Because I say so?" said Norm, even *less* convincingly.

"Oh, well, that's different," said Chelsea. "If you say so, *Norman*, I'll take it down immediately!"

"Really?" said Norm in amazement. He was clearly more masterful than he thought.

"No, not really," said Chelsea flatly.

Norm sighed. He might have known Chelsea was being sarcastic.

"Gimme the money then."

"What?" said Chelsea.

"The twenty pounds," said Norm. "I want it back."

Norm knew that twenty pounds was nowhere near enough compensation for the grief and humiliation he was going to be subjected to at school the next

day. But it was a start. It could at least *begin* to dull the pain. Money, as far as Norm was concerned, was by far the best medicine.

"OK," said Chelsea.

"What?" said Norm.

"You want the twenty pounds back, you can have it."

"Really?" said Norm.

"Nah, not really," said Chelsea. "What are you, *Norman*? Stupid, or something?"

But before Norm could reply, Brian and Dave suddenly tumbled out of the house like a pair of hyperactive chimps.

"We're getting a dog! We're getting a dog!" shrieked Brian.

"Cool!" said Chelsea. "When?"

"Tuesday," said Dave.

"What kind?"

"A cock-a-poo!" said Brian.

Chelsea grinned at Norm. "A cock-a-poo?"

"Yeah," said Norm. "It's like, a cross between a cocker spaniel and a poodle, or something."

"Right," said Chelsea. "Could be worse, I suppose."

"What do you mean?"

"Could be a cross between a shih tzu and a poodle."

shih tzu + poodle = shi....?

Norm didn't want to laugh, but he couldn't help it. It was so annoying.

"We're going to call it The Beatles!" said Dave.

"The Beatles?" said Norm. "What kind of stupid name is that?"

"It's not a stupid name!" said Brian.

"It is for a dog," said Norm.

"The Beatles are Grandpa's favourite band!" said Dave.

"Yeah, so?" said Norm.

"So that's why we're going to call it The Beatles," said Brian, like it was the most logical thing in the world.

"But..." said Norm.

112

"But what?" said Dave.

"Why name it after his favourite band? Why not name it after his favourite cheese?"

Brian pulled a face. "We don't know what his favourite cheese *is*!"

Norm didn't know where to start. So he didn't.

"Well, I think it's a great name," said Chelsea.

You flipping would, thought Norm, pedalling down the drive. But instead of turning round at the bottom and doing another wheelie, Norm just carried on pedalling. **Annoying** girls next door?
Even more annoying little brothers?
Dogs called The Beatles?
Dead expensive bang-up-to-date phones that he was never going to be able to afford in a **year** of Sundays never mind a flipping **month!** Norm felt a sudden overwhelming need to get away and think. And in order to think Norm needed to go somewhere peaceful and quiet. Somewhere like Grandpa's allotment. In fact, somewhere **exactly** like Grandpa's allotment.

CHAPTER 12

Norm opened the gate of the allotments and began pedalling up the path. He loved this place and the fact that it wasn't too neat and tidy. Everything was a bit run down. All the sheds were a bit shabby. Nothing quite matched. It was like the opposite of IKEA. A bit like stepping back in time.

Not that Norm had ever actually stepped back in time before, but he imagined that's what it would feel like if he ever did. Not back to Roman times, or when dinosaurs ruled the earth or anything. Just like maybe, thirty or forty years, or something. Before there were computers and Xboxes and mobile phones. Especially dead expensive, bang-up-to-date mobile phones with loads of apps and stuff.

"Oi! Can't you read?" yelled a strange voice. "No cycling allowed in here!"

So much for flipping peace and quiet, thought Norm, skidding to a halt and getting off his bike. He turned round to see where the voice had come from, only to find Grandpa pushing his wheelbarrow towards him.

"Got you there, didn't I?"

"Yeah, yeah, very funny, Grandpa," mumbled Norm.

"I see someone's got out the wrong side of bed this morning," said Grandpa.

Norm shrugged. Never mind getting out the wrong *side* of bed, he wished he was still *in* bed.

"What's up?" said Grandpa, stopping for a moment. "You've got a face longer than a horse's."

"Oh, you know," said Norm.

"No, I don't actually," said Grandpa. "I'm not psychic."

Norm smiled.

"That's better," said Grandpa, carrying on up the path.

Norm followed, wheeling his bike. What could he say? He couldn't very well tell Grandpa the truth. He probably wouldn't understand anyway. He probably hadn't even heard of Facebook. And even if he **did** understand – and he *had* heard of Facebook, it was way too embarrassing to tell him about the photo. There were some things you just **couldn't** talk to your grandpa about. And this was one of them.

"Come on now, Norman. Spill the beans."

Norm thought for a moment.

"I need a new phone."

"*Need, or want?*"

"Need," said Norm.

Grandpa looked at Norm doubtfully. "Really?"

"Yeah, mine's rubbish," said Norm.

"I see," said Grandpa.

Did Grandpa *really* see, or was he just saying that? wondered Norm. Had he successfully managed to avoid the *real* reason he was so fed up?

"And how much is this phone going to cost, Norman?"

"A lot," said Norm.

"And how much have you got?"

"Not a lot," said Norm.

"Not a lot?" said Grandpa.

"Nothing, actually," said Norm.

"So you want something that costs a lot of money – but you don't actually *have* any money."

Norm nodded. Here it comes, he thought. A speech about how in the olden days if you wanted something you had to save up and how money didn't grow on trees and how kids today were spoilt and blahdy blahdy blah. If Norm had wanted a flipping lecture he'd have stayed at home.

By now they'd reached Grandpa's shed. Grandpa put his wheelbarrow down.

"Well?"

"Well, what, Grandpa?" said Norm.

"What do you think?"

"About what?" said Norm.

"The shed," said Grandpa. "I've pumped it up."

"What?" said Norm.

"I've pumped it up," said Grandpa.

"You mean *pimped* it up," said Norm.

"That's it," said Grandpa. "*Pimped* it up."

Norm looked blankly at the shed.

"What do you think to the colour?"

"Oh, right!" said Norm, suddenly twigging. "You painted it."

"Mint green, they call it."

More like snot green, thought Norm.

"Do you like it?"

"It's great, Grandpa."

"Thanks," said Grandpa. "What else?"

Norm pulled a face. What else? It was just a shed. A common or garden shed. What was this? Spot the flipping difference, or something?

"Erm…" said Norm.

"I mean, what's *really* bothering you?" said Grandpa.

"I told you," said Norm. "I need a new phone."

Grandpa looked at Norm. "I don't believe you."

"What?" said Norm.

"I don't believe you," said Grandpa. "I think there's something else bothering you."

How could Grandpa tell? wondered Norm. Perhaps he really *was* psychic.

"Come on. Spit it out."

Norm didn't want to spit it out. Some things were best left unspat. And this was one of them. "It's a bit..."

"A bit what?" said Grandpa. "Awkward?"

Norm shuffled about, staring at the ground. "That's one word for it."

"Embarrassing?" said Grandpa. "Humiliating?"

"That's two more," said Norm.

Grandpa raised his eyebrows. "Well?"

"Well, what?" said Norm.

"Are you going to tell me or not? I'm growing a beard here."

Norm took a deep breath and slowly exhaled again. "Have you heard of Facebook, Grandpa?"

"Course I've heard of Facebook. Who hasn't?"

"Someone posted a photo of me."

"Oh?" said Grandpa. "And why's that embarrassing?"

"Because I'm totally naked," said Norm.

"Hmm," said Grandpa. "How old are you?"

"Nearly thirteen," said Norm, slightly miffed. Surely Grandpa knew how old he was, didn't he?

"In the photo," said Grandpa.

"Oh, I see," said Norm. "I'm just a baby. But even so..."

"Hmm," said Grandpa again. "And what are you going to do about it?"

"I'm not sure," said Norm.

"Anything else?" said Grandpa.

"Anything else?"

"Apart from the photo and you wanting – sorry, *needing* – a new phone. Anything else you'd like to get off your chest while you're at it?"

"Actually, there *is* something else," said Norm.

Grandpa waited.

"My brothers are getting a dog."

Grandpa pulled a face. "That's it? They're getting a dog?"

"They're going to call it ."

Grandpa's eyes crinkled ever so slightly in the corners. It was the closest he ever came to smiling.

"That's my favourite band ever, that is, Norman."

"Yeah, I know," said Norm. "That's why."

"*I Am The Walrus*," said Grandpa.

"Pardon?" said Norm. Had he heard right? His grandpa was a walrus?

"*Strawberry Fields…Penny Lane…Magical Mystery Tour*. They don't write 'em like that any more."

"Yeah, I know, but you can't call a dog, The Beatles, Grandpa!" said Norm.

"Hmm, yes, that *is* a bit odd, I suppose," said Grandpa.

A ***bit*** odd? thought Norm. It was downright flipping weird, that's what it was!

"They should name it after my *favourite* Beatle."

"Who's that, Grandpa?"

"John Lennon."

"John Lennon?" said Norm. "Cool."

"I'll have a word if you like?" said Grandpa.

"Thanks, Grandpa," said Norm, who knew it would be no good having a word himself. No one ever listened to a flipping word he said.

"It'll cost you though."

Norm smiled.

"I need someone to feed my courgettes while I'm away next weekend."

Norm pulled a face. He'd heard of people feeding

pets for friends and relations while they were away. But *vegetables*?

"Water them," said Grandpa.

"Oh, right, I see," said Norm. "Yeah, no probs, Grandpa."

"Excellent," said Grandpa. "I'll pop round with the keys for the shed and some instructions before I go."

"Instructions?" said Norm. "I know how keys work, Grandpa!"

Grandpa's eyes crinkled. "Not instructions for the keys, you numpty! Instructions on how to feed the courgettes!"

"Oh, right," said Norm.

"You around tomorrow after school?" said Grandpa.

School? thought Norm. Brilliant. Thanks for flipping reminding me, Grandpa!

CHAPTER 13

In the unlikely event of there being a race to school the next day between Norm and an arthritic snail, there would have only been one winner. And it wouldn't have been Norm.

Norm had never been the biggest fan of school. But he knew it was one of those things you had to do. There was no point moaning, even though he often did. You just got on with it, even though he frequently wished he didn't have to. It was a bit like going to the dentist. But less fun. And without the anaesthetic.

What was that old song his mum and dad sang sometimes? wondered Norm, trudging slowly down the street. (Thankfully only *sometimes*, as both his parents had voices like geese with gastroenteritis.) *I Don't Like Mondays.* That was it. Well, Norm wasn't that crazy about Tuesdays or Wednesdays either. Thursdays weren't *too* bad – mainly because the next day was Friday. But Mondays? Mondays were basically evil and should be banned. In fact in the unlikely event of Norm ever becoming prime minister, Norm decided, they flipping well would be.

But this particular Monday looked like it was going to be the daddy of all Mondays. More evil than all the other Mondays rolled into one. Quite simply, this particular Monday could well turn out to be the worst day of Norm's nearly thirteen-year-old life so far. Which was why Norm was approaching school with all the enthusiasm of some old king or queen about to get their head chopped off.

"Norman?" said Mrs Walters, his registration teacher, as Norm walked into class just in the nick of time.

"What?" said Norm.

There were a couple of sniggers. Not the best of starts, thought Norm. Didn't exactly bode well for the rest of the day.

"Are you here?" said Mrs Walters, without looking up from the register.

Norm pulled a face. He'd answered, hadn't he? Course he was flipping here! Where else did she think he was?

"Well?" said Mrs Walters. "I'm waiting."

"Here," muttered Norm sitting down at his desk. "Worst luck."

"For you, or for us, Norman?" said Mrs Walters, finally looking up.

There were a few more sniggers.

"And kindly take your hat and sunglasses off, please."

"What?" said Norm. "Oh yeah. Sorry."

Norm did as he was told and removed his shades and baseball cap. He'd put them on hoping that they might act as some kind of disguise. He'd briefly thought about wearing a false beard as well but had decided against it on the grounds that that may well have attracted *more* attention, not *less* – which would have completely defeated the object. Norm wanted no attention what-so-flipping-ever. He wanted no one to notice him at all. He just wanted the day to end as soon as possible and to be back home.

Mrs Walters carried on taking the register. No one so far, Norm noted, had made any direct reference to the photo. What if no one had actually seen it? What if he'd been worried stupid for no reason whatsoever? What if Chelsea had had a sudden twinge of guilt and taken the photo down from Facebook? Ever so slowly but ever so surely, Norm was beginning to believe that things might – just *might* – not be *quite* so bad after all.

"Norman?" said a voice.

"Yeah?" said Norm, turning round to see Rachel Boon staring at him.

"Oh, it *is* you," said Rachel Boon. "I didn't recognise you with your clothes on."

That did it. The whole class suddenly erupted in gales of laughter. So much for things not being quite so bad after all, thought Norm. It looked like they were about to get even worse!

CHAPTER 14

Norm sat at the back in assembly, doing his best to look inconspicuous. What were those lizard things called? he wondered. The ones that could change colour and blend in with their surroundings? *Chameleons* – that was it. If only he was a chameleon. He could change into the colour of a chair and then no one would notice him at all. The only trouble with that though, thought Norm, was that someone might sit on him. Mind you, if he was a chameleon he wouldn't have to come to school in the first flipping place.

Norm tried to avoid any kind of eye contact. But it was no use. He could still sense people staring at him and nudging each other knowingly. And he didn't need to be psychic to know what they were thinking. This, thought Norm, wasn't turning out to be *as* humiliating as he feared it would be. It was even **more** humiliating than he feared it would be. And not just a *bit* more either. A **lot** more. A whole bunch more. Way off the scale more. This, thought Norm, was humiliation of the very highest order. Humiliation on an entirely different level. A level never previously experienced by a human being. Humiliation which frankly, Norm wouldn't wish on his worst enemy. Not even one of his perfect cousins.

—OF the very highest order
—OF an entirely different le
—More than feared
—High
—Average
—Low

Mikey was waiting in the corridor as everyone filed out of the hall. "Well, that wasn't too bad," he said cheerily as Norm approached.

"What do you mean, not too bad?" said Norm.

134

"I thought everybody was going to be looking at me," said Mikey. "But they weren't."

Norm looked at his friend in disbelief. "Yeah, and you know why that was, don't you?"

"No, why?" said Mikey innocently.

"Because they were all looking at *me*, Mikey, you doughnut!"

"Really?"

"Yeah, really!" said Norm.

"Oh, right," said Mikey. "I did wonder."

"You've got nothing to worry about! You can only see your bum!" said Norm, increasingly exasperated. "You can see my..."

"Come on now, boys. Hurry along to your classes," said the headteacher, breezing past.

"Yes, sir," said Mikey respectfully.

The headteacher carried on for a couple more steps before stopping and turning round. "It's Norman, isn't it?"

"Yes, sir," said Norm.

How come the headteacher knew his name? wondered Norm. There were literally hundreds of kids in the school. He wasn't in any sports teams. He hadn't starred in any shows. He wasn't top of any class. There was no reason why the headteacher should know he even existed, let alone what his flipping name was.

"Thought so," said the headteacher, carrying on down the corridor. "Nice photo by the way."

Norm watched him go before turning to Mikey. "Not too bad, eh?"

Mikey thought for a moment. "Could be worse."

Norm pulled a face. He couldn't see how it could **possibly** be any worse. "You reckon?"

"At least he didn't recognise *me*," said Mikey.

There was a brief silence.

"Just joking, Norm," said Mikey. "Just trying to make you feel a bit better."

"Really?" said Norm. "Could've fooled me."

"Sorry," said Mikey. "I know how you must be feeling."

Norm looked at Mikey in disbelief. "Mikey?"

"Yeah?" said Mikey.

"You have **NO** idea how I'm feeling.

No idea WHAT-SO-FLIPPING-EVER."

Norm set off down the corridor, leaving his best friend standing alone.

"Sorry, Norm," said Mikey.

CHAPTER 15

"You're going to call it **what?**" said Norm, incredulously.

"Him," said Brian.

"**What?**" said Norm, incredulously and with a side order of irritation.

"It's a *him*, not an *it*," said Brian.

Norm sighed. Unusually, all three brothers were sat in the **same** room
                        – on the **same** sofa
                                    – watching television.

"It's just a flipping dog, Brian," said Norm.

"And we can call *him* what we want," said Brian.

Norm had heard some pretty stupid things in his time, but this had to be one of the stupidest. "You can't call a dog *John!*"

"Why not?" said Brian.

"Because...because...because...because..."
"Because of the wonderful things he does!"

                      sang Dave, whose favourite film was *The Wizard Of Oz*.

"Shut up, Dave, you little freak!" hissed Norm.

"I'm not a little freak," said Dave.

"Yeah, you are," said Norm.

"No, I'm not."

"Yeah, you are."

"No, I'm not."

"Yeah, you are."

"Right, I'm telling," said Dave, getting up and setting off in search of the nearest parent.

Norm turned to his middle brother once again. "You just can't call a flipping dog John, and that's all there is to it!"

"That's not a proper reason," said Brian. "And anyway, it was Grandpa's idea."

Norm couldn't argue with that. It *was* Grandpa's idea. But when Grandpa had suggested naming the dog after his favourite member of The Beatles, Norm was pretty sure this wasn't quite what he'd had in mind.

"He meant call it **Lennon**, you doughnut!"

"Him," said Brian. "It's a *him*, not an *it*."

"*Oh, who cares what flipping sex it is?*"
said Norm.

"I'm telling," said Brian.

"Uh?" said Norm.

"You said *sex*!" said Brian. "I'm telling!"

The only thing that was stopping Norm losing the plot altogether was the knowledge that before too long, vengeance would be his. He still hadn't worked out exactly what form the vengeance would take. But he was beginning to get ideas. Ideas that involved hitting Brian where it hurt the most. Not *literally* hitting him where it hurt the most – no matter how tempting that was. And frankly, it was getting more tempting by the second.

"Anyway, it's nothing to do with you, Norman," said Brian defiantly. "We've decided. We're calling him John."

"But..."

"John's a good name."

"It's a perfectly good name," said Norm. "Just not for a dog."

"Why not?" said Brian.

Norm sighed again. "Nothing."

What was the point? Let them call the flipping dog whatever they flipping well wanted. They could call it Microwave, or Buttcheek for all Norm cared. In the great scheme of things it really wasn't that important at all.

And talking of schemes, thought Norm – it was time to get scheming.

CHAPTER 16

Under normal circumstances, Norm arriving home from school to find a slightly whiffy dog curled up fast asleep, not just on the sofa, but in *his* place on the sofa, would have had Norm packing his bags and leaving a note for his parents.

"  " said Brian, putting a finger to his lips.

Under normal circumstances, being told to be quiet by one of his little brothers before he'd even opened his mouth would have annoyed Norm to the point where he would have had to pick up something just so that he could throw it.

But these were far from normal circumstances. School had been no less humiliating for Norm that day than it had been the day before. It still felt like everyone had been looking at him. It still felt like everyone had been whispering behind his back. Not even behind his back. It seemed to Norm that they'd been whispering quite openly in front of him. Not even whispering. Talking quite normally. And sniggering. And pointing. Sometimes sniggering *and* pointing at the same time. Norm could hardly wait to get back home. Nothing that would happen at home could compare to the certain knowledge that the entire school had seen a photo of his dangly bits on Facebook. *And* most probably left a flipping comment. Not that Norm had the slightest intention of reading any of them. So by comparison, finding a slightly whiffy dog in his place on the sofa almost came as a relief.

"He's stressed out," said Brian quietly.

He's stressed out? thought Norm. The **dog** was stressed out? What had a flipping **dog** got to be stressed out about? A worldwide bone shortage?

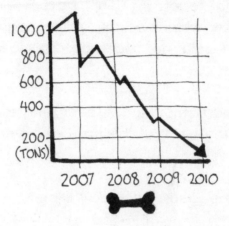

A new law making it illegal to pee on lamp posts?

A cat moving in next door?

"Wish he'd wake up so we can play with him," said Dave.

"We've got to let him sleep, Dave," said Brian. "Remember what the lady at the dogs' home said? She said he might be traumatised by the journey."

"Yeah," said Norm. "Must've been *really* traumatic sitting in the back of the car being stroked for ten minutes."

"Are you being sarcastic?" said Brian.

"No," said Norm, sarcastically.

"Sarcasm is the lowest form of humour."

"No, really?" said Norm, even more sarcastically.

"He's been deprived of love and human affection," said Brian. "He might be mentally scarred."

"Or he might just be tired," said Dave.

"Shut up, Dave," said Brian.

"I'm just saying," said Dave.

"Well, don't," said Brian.

The dog suddenly twitched slightly and whimpered softly, but didn't wake up.

"So cute," said Dave.

"You reckon?" said Norm, for whom the newest member of the family was about as cute as eczema and even more unwelcome. At least you could get flipping cream for eczema.

"He's probably dreaming," said Brian.

What of? wondered Norm. Not being thrown out of a supermarket for being stood naked in the nine items or less checkout with ten items – that was for flipping sure.

"Boys?" said Norm's mum, appearing in the doorway. "What did I tell you about not letting John sit on the furniture?"

"Aw, Mum, he's tired!" said Brian.

"He's been caramelised by the journey," said Dave.

"Traumatised, Dave, you idiot," said Brian.

"Mum, Brian just called me an idiot," whined Dave, like Norm's mum hadn't been there at the time.

"What's your point?" said Norm.

Either unaware of the bickering or choosing to ignore it, Norm's mum looked at the dog and smiled sweetly. "Ah, bless," she said.

Norm pulled a face. "You're not going to make it get off then?"

"What's that, love?"

"You're just going to let it stay there?"

"*Him!*" said Brian. "It's a *him!*"

"Well, Mum?" said Norm, ignoring Brian. "Are you?"

Norm's mum thought for a moment. "It does seem rather a shame to wake him."

"Thanks, Mum!" said Brian.

Norm was dumbstruck with the utter unfairness of it all. What kind of signal was this sending out to his brothers? Why tell them they couldn't do something and then let them flipping well do it? If it had been **him** who'd been told not to sit on the sofa and he had done, there would have been no second chance. He'd have been grounded immediately. Or banned from something or other. Or had his pocket money stopped or something. Not that he ever *got* any flipping pocket money these days! But that wasn't the point, thought Norm. The point was: where was the consistency? How come there was one rule for his stupid little brothers and another rule for him?

"Just this once though," said Norm's mum a bit more sternly. "If there's any mess, your dad'll go bonkers."

Hmm, thought Norm, the cogs of his mind already whirring into action. He will, won't he?

But there was no time for the seeds of whatever scheme just beginning to sprout in Norm's head to sprout any further, because at that moment everyone suddenly became aware of a quite nauseating and revolting smell filling the room. Everyone that is, except for the dog, which remained steadfastly asleep.

"Norman!" said Norm's mum, wrinkling her nose and wafting a hand in front of her face.

"What?" said Norm innocently.

"Do you have to?"

"It wasn't me, Mum, it was the dog!" protested Norm, who under normal circumstances would have been proud to own up to such a humdinger of a trouser cough. But these were far from normal circumstances. The flipping dog had only been in the house five flipping minutes and already Norm was being blamed for something *it* had done! It was bad enough being blamed for stuff that Brian and Dave had done. Norm was used to that. But a flipping dog? How unfair was *that*?

But actually, thought Norm, eyeing the dog, still curled up fast asleep on the sofa – it was OK. So-called John was going to come in very handy when it came to wreaking revenge on Brian. And so was the sofa.

CHAPTER 17

The question as far as Norm was concerned, wasn't whether or not to deliberately mess up the sofa. The question as far as Norm was concerned, was *how* to deliberately mess up the sofa. Spread a bit of you-know-what on it? Canine you-know-what of course, as opposed to human. Human you-know-what came in too many different consistencies. And just like butter, some was more spreadable than others.

Not that Norm had ever tried spreading human you-know-what on a sofa before. Or anywhere else for that matter. But canine you-know-what had a distinct and unique smell all of its own. It couldn't easily be mistaken for any other kind. Feline you-know-what for instance, which, according to Grandpa, not only remained undetected for days on end because cats buried it rather than leaving it for people to tread in, but also played havoc with his chrysanthemums. Either way though, decided Norm, deliberately messing up the sofa with you-know-what – canine or otherwise – was just a bit *too* messy and frankly, a bit *too* gross. The potential for it to go spectacularly pear-shaped was just too great. And besides, Norm liked to think he had his standards.

Peeing on the sofa was a possibility. Well, perhaps not actually peeing on it. Norm wasn't sure he could trust himself to stop once he'd started. And of course there was always a chance of being caught in the act, like the time he was caught peeing in his dad's wardrobe – or technically, the time he was caught *about* to pee in his dad's wardrobe. No, thought Norm. It was probably better to pee in some kind of container – and then pour a bit onto the sofa. But how much? How much did dogs actually pee? It wasn't something

Norm had ever spent much time thinking about. Or *any time* thinking about actually. Once again he decided that the risk was just a bit too great. Peeing on the sofa wasn't really an option after all. There had to be another way. A not quite so risky way. A way which wouldn't immediately arouse suspicion.

Norm waited until everyone had gone to bed that night before creeping back downstairs. The dog was curled up fast asleep again, not on the sofa but next to the radiator in the kitchen. A proper dog basket had been ordered from one of the shopping channels by Norm's mum, but in the meantime she'd folded up a blanket and stuffed it inside a cardboard box. The dog certainly wasn't complaining. It looked so cosy and content, thought Norm. As if it hadn't got a care in the world.

Which it clearly hadn't. It was so flipping unfair. Norm had currently got more cares than he cared to think about – how to get his own back on Brian being the most pressing – and how to get his hands on a dead expensive, bang-up-to-date phone like Danny's not far behind.

As Norm looked on, the dog stirred slightly, scratched itself behind its ear and promptly fell back asleep again. Did dogs ever shed their coats? wondered Norm. And if so, when? Did it only happen at certain times of the year? Like autumn or something? Because, if so, finding dog hair on his precious sofa would be a sure-fire way to annoy his dad – and with luck may even hasten his departure. The dog's departure, thought Norm. Not his dad's.

But time was of the essence. Norm couldn't afford to hang around for nature to take its course. He might just have to intervene and give nature a helping hand. But how? How best to harvest dog hair? Not by simply yanking a fistful out, that was for sure. The dog would almost certainly wake up and bark the house down. It wouldn't be difficult with walls the thickness of toilet paper.

As Norm mulled over this latest conundrum he happened to glance at the notice board hanging on the wall above the radiator. There, among the birthday party invitations for his brothers, the telephone numbers written on scraps of paper and letters from school, was a photo. It was a photo of Norm's mum and dad when they were much younger. Norm's dad had long hair and a beard and looked a bit like Jesus. Except that as far as Norm knew Jesus didn't have glasses and never wore a T-shirt with *Iron Maiden* written on it.

And then it suddenly hit Norm. His dad didn't have a beard any more. As far as he could remember he hadn't had a beard in all the nearly thirteen years he'd known him. The occasional few days' worth of stubble, yes. But a full-blown beard? Never. And why not? Because he shaved, that's why not. And what did he use to shave with? Genius, thought Norm, heading for the bathroom. Sheer flipping genius.

Norm was back downstairs in seconds flat, clutching his dad's razor. But now what? Norm had never shaved himself before – let alone a dog. He'd seen his dad do it. Shave himself, that is – not a dog. His dad covered his face in foam first. Should Norm cover the dog in foam first? Or at least, should he cover the bit of the dog he intended to shave in foam first? Actually that was a point. Which bit of the dog should he shave?

The dog began to stir again. If Norm didn't hurry up and do it soon it would wake up and his plan would be in tatters. But then, as if sensing Norm's dilemma, it obligingly rolled onto its back and stretched luxuriously. This was it. The opportunity Norm had been waiting for. Without further ado he began shaving an area of the dog's stomach close to one of its hind legs, but sufficiently far away enough from its middle leg. If he got too close to *that*, the dog would wake the whole flipping street up, never mind the house. It wasn't easy. Norm decided that as soon as he was old enough to shave – he wouldn't. He'd grow a beard instead. Maybe even wear a T-shirt with *Iron Maiden* written on it.

All of a sudden, Norm – and the dog – were bathed in a bright, white light. Like prisoners on the run being lit up by a helicopter searchlight. He'd been caught in the act.

"It's not what it seems," said Norm. But even as he said it, Norm realised it was a ridiculous thing to say. It was *exactly* how it seemed. He was shaving a dog.

But there was no reply. Norm spun round to see the fridge door open. That would explain the light then, thought Norm.

"Dave?" said Norm, shielding his eyes. "Is that you?"

It *was* Dave. And knowing Norm's little brother he'd already be figuring out how this situation could best be used to his advantage. Norm decided to get in there first. "I'll give you my old phone when I get a new one," said Norm.

Dave didn't say anything.

"As long as you don't tell Mum and Dad."

Dave still didn't say anything.

"You didn't see anything, right?"

Dave *still* didn't say anything.

"Deal, Dave?" said Norm. "You don't say anything and you get my old phone?"

They looked at each other for a moment before Dave eventually closed the fridge door again, plunging Norm and the dog back into semi-darkness.

"I'll take that as a 'yes' then," muttered Norm, as Dave padded towards the stairs.

CHAPTER 18

Of all the sounds Norm would have liked to have been woken by the next morning, the sound of the vacuum cleaner was probably the one he would have liked to have been woken by the least.

"Morning, love," said Norm's mum, cheerily, as Norm walked through the front-room door, yawning and scratching his backside.

"Morning," said Norm, not quite so cheerily.

"That was lucky," said Norm's mum, unplugging the vacuum cleaner.

What was lucky? thought Norm.

Scratching his backside?

"Finding that dog hair on the sofa before your dad did!"

Norm sighed wearily. "Oh, right."

"He'd have gone bonkers if he'd seen it."

"That was the whole flipping point," muttered Norm under his breath.

Norm's mum pulled a face. "What did you say?"

Oops, thought Norm. Some things were best left unsaid. And that had been one of them. It was so flipping annoying though. Had his mum got any idea how much trouble he'd gone to, shaving the dog? Obviously not.

"Er, I said 'good point, Mum'."

"Oh, well," said Norm's mum. "I might as well carry on cleaning now, I suppose."

Norm looked at his mum anxiously. "Are the

cousins coming?"

"No," laughed Norm's mum.

"Thank goodness for that," said Norm, imagining all the weird food he now wouldn't have to eat.

"Ah, don't be so rotten, love," said Norm's mum, giving Norm a look.

"They're so annoying," said Norm.

"I know you're not being serious."

"I'm being totally serious."

"Well, that's a shame."

"Why?" said Norm.

"Because it's our turn to go there this weekend. Remember?"

"  " wailed Norm.

What with everything else going on, Norm had completely forgotten about the proposed visit to see his perfect cousins. Either that or he'd managed to block it out of his mind. And by not thinking about it, he'd somehow convinced himself that it wasn't actually going to happen. But now it appeared that it was.

"It'll be nice!" said Norm's mum.

"No, it won't," said Norm.

"It will."

"It won't."

"How do you know?"

"I just do."

Norm's mum paused. Like she had an ace up her sleeve and it was time to play it.

"Ed will be there."

"Will he?" said Norm.

Norm's mum nodded.

"Well, that's different then."

"Really?" said Norm's mum brightly.

"Nah," said Norm. "Not really."

Norm's mum's face fell. For a moment Norm almost felt bad for building her hopes up. But it soon passed.

"I thought he was climbing Mount Kajagoogoo."

"Kilimanjaro," corrected Norm's mum.

"Yeah, that," said Norm.

"He's back," said Norm's mum.

"Oh, goody," said Norm.

"Breakfast!" yelled Norm's dad from the kitchen.

Norm showed no sign of moving.

"Go on, love," said Norm's mum. "You don't want to be late for school now, do you?"

That's what you think, thought Norm, trudging slowly towards the door. He'd absolutely *love* to be late for school.

CHAPTER 19

"Table for one?" said Norm's dad in a rubbish French accent, ushering Norm towards the table as soon as he entered the kitchen.

Norm didn't even bother trying to summon up a smile. Not only had his cunning plan to sabotage the sofa proved to be not quite so cunning as he'd thought, he'd just been reminded he was going to see all three of his perfect cousins in a few days' time. Providing one of them wasn't working on a cure for all known diseases or crossing the Sahara Desert on a flipping pogo stick or whatever. And besides, he'd heard his dad's so-called 'joke' a billion times before. And it wasn't funny the first time.

"You're full of the joys of spring," said Norm's dad. "What's the matter?"

"Nothing," said Norm, sitting down and helping himself to a bowl of supermarket own-brand coco pops.

"Yes, there is. I can tell. Come on, son. What's up?"

"How long have you got?" muttered Norm.

"All day," said Norm's dad.

It was true. Norm's dad wasn't working any more. Not that Norm was ever very sure what he did when he *was* working. He knew he worked for a company that made stuff. What kind of stuff? Norm had no idea. It could have been solar-powered nose-hair clippers for all he knew. Or cared for that matter.

"Well?" said Norm's dad. "I'm waiting."

"Where do I start?" said Norm.

Luckily Norm didn't *have* to start, because at that moment his brothers exploded into the kitchen, closely followed by the dog. Unlike the dog however, Brian and Dave managed to stop. The dog *tried* to stop but merely succeeded in skittering and skidding across the floor, nearly knocking Norm's dad clean off his feet in the process. There was a brief pause. How was Dad going to react? wondered Norm. Hopefully, very badly. For the dog's sake anyway.

Norm watched as the dog looked pleadingly up at Norm's dad, tongue lolling like freshly sliced ham and dribbling all over the floor.

This was looking promising, thought Norm. With every passing second, the chances of the dog being taken back to the dogs' home and Brian having to spend the rest of his life in therapy were increasing. At this rate Norm wouldn't actually have to do anything himself.

Norm's dad suddenly burst out laughing.

What? thought Norm. This wasn't supposed to happen.

"Sit, John!" said Brian.

Not only did the dog *not* sit, it started whizzing round in ever decreasing circles trying to catch its tail. Or rather, what remained of its tail, since technically, it didn't have one.

Norm's dad laughed even louder.

Norm couldn't believe it. What could his dad possibly find in the least bit amusing about being crashed into by an out-of-control four-legged saliva machine? If it had been *him* crashing into his dad, his dad would've gone ballistic. It was so flipping unfair.

"Sit, John!" said Brian again – with about as much effect as the first time.

"Looks like someone needs a spot of training," chuckled Norm's dad.

Norm presumed he was referring to the dog and not Brian, though frankly nothing would have surprised him by now.

"Find out if there's a class you can take him to locally and I'll pay for it."

"Thanks, Dad!" sang Brian and Dave together.

Hmm, interesting, thought Norm. So his dad was in a good mood, was he? In that case now might be a good time to ask if he could have a new phone. Which reminded Norm. He needed a quiet word with Dave.

Norm waited for his dad to busy himself at the sink and for Brian to feed the dog.

"*Pssst!*" hissed Norm as Dave sat down and helped himself to a bowl of own-brand coco pops.

Dave looked up to see Norm shushing him by holding an index finger to his lips.

"What?" said Dave.

Norm mimed pulling a zip across his mouth and then mimed holding an imaginary phone to his ear.

By now Dave was looking distinctly puzzled. But then Norm never had been much good at mime.

"The dog!" whispered Norm.

"What about him?" whispered Dave.

"Last night!" hissed Norm, miming shaving with an imaginary razor.

Dave pulled a face.

"You didn't see anything, right?"

"Didn't see what?" said Dave. "What are you on about?"

It suddenly dawned on Norm. His little brother really *hadn't* seen anything the night before. He knew nothing about Norm's offer to give him his old phone. Dave must've been sleepwalking!

"Doesn't matter," said Norm quickly.

"What doesn't matter?" said Norm's dad, turning round.

"Nothing, Dad," said Norm casually.

Norm's dad looked at Norm. "Nothing doesn't matter?"

"Yes. I mean, no," said Norm.

"Either it does, or it doesn't," said Norm's dad.

"It doesn't," said Norm.

Norm smiled. He'd got away with it. He'd shaved the dog and no one was any wiser. Apart from the dog. And the dog wasn't going to say anything. Hopefully, anyway.

As if reading Norm's mind, the dog suddenly turned round and stared at Norm. Norm had a sudden feeling that John was going to go for him. Maybe even take a chunk out of him.

"Stay, boy," said Norm anxiously.

The dog did the complete opposite and went.

"Come on, Dave," said Brian, heading for the door. "Let's go after him."

"Coming," said Dave, following his brother and the dog, and leaving Norm and his dad alone in the kitchen.

"Dad?" said Norm, keen to find out whether his dad was still feeling generous.

"What?"

"Can I get a new phone, please?"

Norm's dad looked at Norm. "You're not serious, are you?"

Norm thought for a moment. Was this a trick question? Course he was flipping serious. Why wouldn't he be flipping serious? He wanted a new phone. No – forget that. He *needed* a new phone.

"You think I'm made of money?" said Norm's dad.

"But..."

"What planet are you living on, Norman?"

"The same one as you, unfortunately," muttered Norm under his breath.

"What was that?" said Norm's dad.

"Nothing," said Norm.

CHAPTER 20

Saturday dawned bright and clear and without a single cloud in the sky. Birds sang. Babies gurgled. Children played. All was well with the world. Unless, that is, you happened to be Norm. Which Norm did.

Norm, it's fair to say, was not a happy bunny. Even by unhappy bunny standards Norm was not a happy bunny. Not only was he being dragged off against his will to see his perfect cousins, he was pretty sure he'd be dragged off on another pointless walk with them as well.

"So?" said Norm's dad with no hint of a rubbish French accent as Norm entered the kitchen and helped himself to a bowl of own-brand coco pops.

"So, *what*?" said Norm.

"You never did tell me why you want a new phone. What's wrong with the one you've got?"

Norm looked at his dad like he'd just stepped off a spaceship from the planet Doughnut. But as Norm's dad was at the sink doing the washing-up and had his back to Norm, it had no noticeable effect.

"What's *wrong* with it?" said Norm.

"Yeah," said Norm's dad.

"What's *right* with it, more like?"

"Can you make calls with it?"

"Yes, of course, Dad," said Norm with barely concealed impatience.

"Can you *receive* calls with it?"

Norm sighed. "Yes, Dad."

"Can you send and receive texts with it?"

"Yes, Dad, but..."

"So what's the problem?"

What's the problem? thought Norm. Having a flipping dinosaur for a dad! *That's* what the flipping problem was!

"As long as we can get in touch with you and you can get in touch with us that's all that matters," said Norm's dad.

In Victorian times maybe, thought Norm, to whom a phone's capacity to send and receive calls and texts ranked somewhat lower than having good-quality graphics and a decent mp3 player.

"As long as we know you're safe."

"Whatever," said Norm.

"No, Norman. Not whatever," said Norm's dad. "There *are* no whatevers when it comes to personal safety."

"But..."

"And there are no buts either," said Norm's dad. "We'll just have to agree to differ."

No, we flipping won't, thought Norm.

"If it was broken, that would be a different matter," said Norm's dad, still busy at the sink.

Norm didn't say anything. His mind had just gone from 0–60 in 2.4 seconds. A new personal best.

"Norman?"

"Yeah, Dad?" said Norm innocently.

"Don't even think about it."

Norm's dad turned round and smiled. He knew perfectly well Norm was *already* thinking about it.

"I can read you like a book."

In that case, thought Norm, he wished his dad would hurry up and flipping finish it. He was desperate to know what was going to happen.

It was then that Norm noticed his dad's face was the same colour as an orang-utan's rear end.

"Why are you blushing, Dad?"

"I'm not blushing."

"Yeah, you are!" said Norm. "You're bright red!"

"What are you talking about?" said Norm's dad, grabbing a saucepan lid from the draining board and using it as a mirror to check his reflection. "Oh yeah, so I am. How funny."

"Funny?" said Norm. He couldn't see how having a face the colour of an orang-utan's rear end could be considered funny. It usually meant you were dead embarrassed about something. Having a photo of you stark naked posted on Facebook for instance. Norm gave a little shudder as an image of a photo of his *dad* stark naked posted on Facebook flashed through his mind.

"Not *funny* funny," said Norm's dad. "*Odd* funny."

"Right," said Norm.

"Must be some kind of allergic reaction,"

What to? thought Norm. The twenty-first century?

"Your mum's using a new perfume."

Norm looked puzzled.

"Why would that…"

Norm stopped suddenly as he put two and two together and figured what his dad had meant.

"Aw, Dad – that is so gross!"

"What?" grinned Norm's dad. "You think your mum and I don't have a little cuddle now and then?"

"Seriously, Dad. Stop!" said Norm, fairly certain that if this conversation carried on much longer he'd lose what little breakfast he'd managed to get down his neck so far.

"Could just be from shaving," said Norm's dad, still studying his reflection in the saucepan lid and tilting his head to get the best angle.

Oops, thought Norm, alarm bells immediately beginning to ring. "Shaving, Dad?"

"Yeah."

"Shaving what?"

Norm's dad turned to Norm. "My face, Norman."

"Right," said Norm.

"What else do you think I shave?"

Norm gave another little shudder. He really didn't like to think what else his dad might shave, so it was best not to.

"I should maybe change the razor blade."

Good idea, thought Norm. If only *he'd* thought of doing that.

CHAPTER 21

Despite having to call at the doctor's on the way, they still managed to get to Norm's perfect cousins only a couple of minutes later than originally planned. Norm had been hoping that the unexpected detour might have delayed them. In fact, in his wildest dreams Norm had been hoping that his dad's rash might have led to the cancellation of the trip altogether. But sadly it wasn't to be. He'd just been prescribed some cream. They'd collected the cream from the chemist's. By the time they arrived, Norm's dad's face had returned to its original colour. The rash had disappeared. Some people were just so inconsiderate.

"I'd given you up for lost," said Auntie Jem, appearing at the door.

No such flipping luck, thought Norm.

"Sorry, Jemma," said Norm's mum. "We should have phoned."

"Yes, you should," said Auntie Jem frostily.

"Alan got a rash on his…"

"But as it happens we're running a bit late ourselves what with Becky's rehearsals and my personal trainer getting a puncture."

Norm pulled a face. How could a personal trainer get a puncture?

"Not to mention Ed playing piano at the old folks' home."

But you still flipping *did* mention it, thought Norm. It really was quite incredible. They'd only been there thirty seconds and already he felt like screaming.

"It's nice of you to fit us in, Jemma," said Norm's dad with more than a hint of sarcasm. But Auntie Jem didn't notice because at that moment the dog bounded through the door and crashed into her, sending her sprawling backwards. The only reason she didn't fall over was because she managed to grab hold of the telephone table in the hallway, but in doing so she knocked over a vase, which promptly smashed on the floor.

It was by far the funniest thing that Norm had seen all day. Come to think of it, thought Norm, it was the *only* funny thing he'd seen all day.

"Sit, John!" said Brian.

Far from sitting, the dog simply carried on and bombed headlong up the stairs, narrowly avoiding crashing into Uncle Steve coming down in the opposite direction.

"Whoa! What was *that*?" he said.

"John," said Brian.

"John?" said Uncle Steve.

"After John Lennon," said Brian.

"He's a cock-a-poo," said Dave.

"A what-a-poo?" said Uncle Steve.

"A cock-a-poo," said Brian. "A cross between a cocker spaniel and a poodle."

"Oh, I see," said Uncle Steve. "Cool."

"It's *not* cool at all, Steven!" said Auntie Jem, dusting herself down. "Look what it's done!"

"Not *it*," said Brian. "*Him*."

"That's a very expensive vase, that is!" said Auntie Jem, ignoring Brian.

Was a very expensive vase, thought Norm.

"I'm sure I've seen one like that in IKEA,"

said Norm's mum.

Auntie Jem looked at Norm's mum like she was something she'd just scraped off the bottom of her shoe. "I can assure you, you have *not* seen a vase like that in IKEA, Linda! That's from Africa, that is!"

Was from Africa, thought Norm. And if it was so precious then surely it should be in a museum and not on a flipping telephone table. That was asking for trouble, that was. And anyway, thought Norm, what was wrong with IKEA? He didn't particularly like going there himself. In fact he hated going there himself. But he hated the way Auntie Jem spoke so sneerily to his mum even more.

"Come on, Jem," said Uncle Steve. "It was an accident! He didn't mean to do it. He's just a dog for goodness' sake!"

"He's been fossilised," said Dave.

"Fossilised?" said Uncle Steve.

"He means *traumatised*," explained Brian.

"Right," said Uncle Steve as Norm's oldest cousin, Ed, appeared in the doorway wearing a T-shirt with *Tanzania* written on it.

"Hi, Ed," said Norm's mum, keen to change the subject. "How was your trip?"

"Awesome, thanks, Auntie Linda," said Ed.

"Wish you were still there?"

"Yeah," said Ed.

That makes two of us, thought Norm.

"Cool T-shirt," said Dave. "Where d'ya get it?"

Norm looked at his youngest brother. "Where do you *think* he got it, Dave, you doughnut? Belgium?"

"Now, now, Norman," said Norm's dad. "There's no need for that."

But as far as Norm was concerned, there was *every* need for that. It was just showing off. Why did Ed have to have a T-shirt with the name of somewhere on the front, just because he'd flipping been there? Norm had a good mind to get one with *The Shops* written on it. Or *Toilet*.

"What I thought we'd do," said Uncle Steve, also quite keen to change the subject, "is go for a walk first and then come back here for a bite to eat. How does that sound?"

"Terrific," said Norm's dad.

Like my worst nightmare, thought Norm.

"Come on, guys! We're leaving!" Uncle Steve called up the stairs.

"Do I have to come, Dad?" called Norm's cousin, Danny, from the landing.

"Yes, of course you do, Dan! Why?"

"I was hoping to study."

Norm's mum and Norm exchanged a quick glance, both knowing full well that Norm wouldn't voluntarily study unless the future of civilisation was at stake. And frankly even then it would depend on what was on TV.

"Hear that, love? Danny wants to study." Norm's mum paused for effect. "Actually *wants* to study."

Yeah, yeah, whatever, thought Norm, who had a pretty good idea *why* Danny wanted to study. So that he could get straight A's in his next report –

without having to fake it! What was the deal this time? An even *more* dead expensive, bang-up-to-date phone? Unless of course Danny was just looking for an excuse not to go on a walk? And who could blame him if he was, thought Norm, who at that precise moment would have given pretty much anything not to be going on a walk.

Including money. Not that Norm actually **had** any money.

"He's *so* cute!" cooed Becky in a squeaky baby voice as she appeared, cradling the dog in her arms.

"He's called John," said Brian.

"He's a cock-a-poo," said Dave.

But Becky wasn't listening. She'd put the dog down on the floor and was busy tickling its tummy. "You like that, don't you? Yes you do!"

The dog clearly did like that and had rolled onto its back, stretching out luxuriously and whimpering softly.

"Ooh, look," said Becky.

"What?" said Brian.

"He's got a little bald patch. Almost like he's been shaved."

"Oh yeah," said Dave. "Just near his..."

"But—" began Norm's dad.

"Here, boy! Walkies!" said Norm, cutting his dad off and heading down the path.

Norm's mum gave Norm a quizzical look.

"What?" said Norm.

"You actually *want* to go for a walk?"

"Yeah, course," said Norm. "What's so funny about that?"

CHAPTER 22

"How's it going?" said Danny cheerily, catching up with Norm and walking alongside him.

"All right, I suppose," said Norm, slightly less cheerily.

"You suppose?" said Danny.

"Yeah, well, you know," shrugged Norm.

They were in the park. Brian and Dave had trotted off ahead with Becky and the dog. Norm saw that Ed was lagging behind with the grown-ups, though not nearly as far behind as he would have liked. But then Ed could have been on the other side of the planet – and he *still* wouldn't have been as far behind as

Norm would have liked. He was so flipping perfect with his stupid flipping T-shirt, he actually made Danny and Becky look quite normal.

"So what's new?" said Danny.

"Not much," said Norm.

" 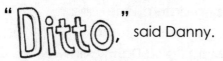," said Danny.

Norm pulled a face.

"It means the same," said Danny.

So why not just flipping say that then? thought Norm. Why try and be cool and start speaking flipping Icelandic, or whatever flipping language it was?

"It's Latin," said Danny, as if he'd read Norm's mind.

"Latin?" said Norm. "You actually speak Latin?"

Danny shrugged. "Enough to get by."

Get by where? thought Norm. Ancient flipping Rome?

"More like the odd word really," said Danny.

Norm could think of a couple of odd words he'd like
to say himself. And not in flipping Latin either. But
at that moment Danny's dead expensive,
bang-up-to-date phone rang.

"Hi, Mum," said Danny, answering.

Norm tried not to stare at the
phone, but it wasn't easy. It was
like...like... Norm couldn't quite
think what it was like. But it was
definitely like something.

"He's what?" said Danny. "Teaching Auntie Linda
and Uncle Alan some Swahili?"

Danny turned to Norm and shook his head. "Kuh!
What's Ed like, eh?"

Norm nodded and smiled through gritted teeth. He
knew precisely what Ed was like – but it was probably
best not to say.

"No, I won't forget, Mum," said Danny.
"'Kay, Mum. Bye."

"Forget what?" said Norm,
instantly regretting asking.

"Capoeira," said
Danny, pocketing his
phone again.

"What's that?"
said Norm without
thinking – instantly
wishing he could
rewind and delete
the question. He had no
interest whatsoever in finding
out what flipping capoeira was. He couldn't
care less what flipping capoeira was. Why on
earth had he even asked?

"It's a Brazilian art form that combines elements
of martial arts, sports and music, created by
descendants of African slaves in the sixteenth
century."

"Just testing," said Norm. "I knew that."

Danny looked at Norm and smiled.

"What?" said Norm.

"Nothing," said Danny.

But Norm knew perfectly well what Danny was smiling at. He was smiling because he knew that Norm was just pretending that he knew what

Capo-flipping-what's-it was.

Worse still, Norm was pretty sure Danny knew that Norm knew that he knew he was just pretending he knew what capo-flipping-what's-it was.

"So have you got to go then?" said Norm.

"Where to?" said Danny.

"Cappuccino," said Norm.

Danny smiled. "You mean, capoeira?"

"Whatever," said Norm.

"No, not yet."

Norm pulled a face. What was the point of Danny's mum reminding him then? Apart from showing off? Actually, thought Norm, there was no point apart from showing off. Typical Auntie Jem, really.

They rounded a corner to see Norm's brothers and Becky waiting while the dog cocked its leg and peed on a lamp post.

"Aw," said Becky. "That is so sad!"

No, it wasn't, thought Norm. It had to pee somewhere, didn't it? What was it supposed to do? Wait till they got home and then pee in the toilet like everyone else?

It was only when he got closer that Norm realised Becky was actually looking at a poster stuck to the lamp post and that on the poster was a photo of a dog.

"Lost," read Brian. "Goldie, the golden retriever. Much-loved family pet.'

Goldie the golden retriever, much-loved family pet

"Goldie?" said Dave. "That's a rubbish name!"

Unlike John, thought Norm.

"And look," said Brian. "There's a reward!"

"Ooh!" said Dave. "Wonder how much?"

Hmm, yeah, I wonder, thought Norm, suddenly experiencing the familiar tingle of cogs whirring into action.

"I wouldn't expect a reward," said Brian.

Speak for yourself, you little freak, thought Norm.

"My reward would be the satisfaction of knowing I'd helped reunite man with man's best friend."

"That's sexist," said Danny.

Dave gasped in horror.

"What's wrong with that?" said Danny. "I just said sexist."

Dave gasped again.

"Shut up, Dave," said Norm.

"Nice photo by the way, Norman," said Becky, without turning round.

Norm looked. It was an OK kind of photo, as photos of dogs went. Nothing out of the ordinary though. It certainly wouldn't win any prizes.

"You reckon?"

Becky looked at Norm and smiled. "Not that photo, silly."

The penny suddenly dropped. Norm immediately began to feel himself blushing. Like he'd just been simmering

and now all of a sudden he'd been turned all the way up to gas mark 5. He knew precisely which photo Becky meant.

"It's so sweet," said Becky.

"Why have you gone red?"
said Dave.

But Norm didn't reply. He was staring at Brian in much the same way that a spider stares at a fly just before it strikes.

"What?" said Brian. "Why are you looking at me like that?"

"Just thinking," said Norm.

"What about?" said Brian.

"That's for you to know and me to find out," said Norm.

Brian pulled a face. "Shouldn't that be the other way round?"

"What?" said Norm.

"Shouldn't that be 'for me to know and you to find out'?"

"Whatever," said Norm.

Without warning, another dog suddenly came bounding along, prompting John to shoot off across the park like a rocket.

"Stay, John!" yelled Brian.

As usual John didn't take the slightest bit of notice to any kind of command, but as the other dog was about three times his size it was hardly surprising.

"Równaj!" yelled a voice. "Równaj!"

The other dog immediately stopped in its tracks, turned round and started trotting back towards the owner of the voice – a girl roughly the same age as Norm. Bizarrely, so did John.

"Siad!" said the girl.

Both dogs dutifully sat down.

"Oh, hi, Kasia!" said Danny.

"Hello, Danny," said the girl, with a strong, eastern European accent.

"Kasia's from my school," said Danny, turning to Norm. "She's Polish."

"So's John by the looks of things," laughed Becky.

"What?" said Brian.

"Say something else," said Becky to Kasia. "In Polish. Some kind of command."

"Stój," said Kasia, pointing at John. "Stój."

"What does that mean?" said Dave.

"It means 'stay'," said Kasia, walking away a few paces before turning around again.

Sure enough, John stayed rooted to the spot.

"Domnie!" said Kasia, slapping her thighs.

John jumped up straightaway and ran towards Kasia.

"Dobry pies!" said Kasia, patting John vigorously. John, meanwhile, responded by barking and furiously wagging the remains of his tail.

"'Domnie' means 'come'?" said Brian.

"And 'dobry pies' means 'good dog'," said Kasia.

"So John only understands Polish!" said Dave.

"That's amazing!"

"What's so amazing about that?" said Norm.

"Well, do you understand Polish?" said Dave.

"No, but..."

"Well then," said Dave.

Norm thought about saying something else, but didn't. His mind was elsewhere. There was an opportunity to make money here. Possibly even enough money to buy a dead expensive, bang-up-to-date phone! All he had to do was somehow arrange for John to get 'lost'. He'd figure out the rest later. And the best part? Not only would he get his new phone with the reward money, Brian would be devastated. Which would serve him flipping well right for giving the photo to Chelsea. Vengeance would finally be Norm's!

"Come on, guys," said Becky, heading off. "I've got stuff to do."

"Ditto," said Norm, following.

CHAPTER 23

"Norman?" said Norm's mum.

There was no reply from Norm. Norm's mum nudged him with her elbow.

"What?" said Norm irritably, taking his headphones off.

"How many times have I told you not to listen to your iPod while we're eating?"

Norm thought for a moment. "Er, twice now, Mum."

"Don't answer your mother back!" said Norm's dad.

"But..."

"No buts, Norman!" said Norm's dad. *"Don't* answer back!"

Norm pulled a face. He'd been asked a question and then told not to flipping answer it! Imagine if that happened at school. A teacher asked what the square-whatsit of some random number was – and then told you not to answer it! It was ridiculous.

"Sorry, everyone," said Norm's dad. "Most embarrassing."

You call *that* embarrassing? thought Norm. Try having your flipping dangleberries plastered all over Facebook! Now *that's* flipping embarrassing!

"Delicious soup by the way, Becky," said Norm's dad. "What is it again?"

"Cream of fennel," said Becky.

Cream of fennel? thought Norm, taking a sip. Cream of flipping flannel more like.

"You really must give me the recipe," said Norm's dad.

You really mustn't, thought Norm.

"Wait till you see what Becky's made for main course," beamed Auntie Jem.

"Well?" said Norm's dad expectantly.

"Oh, it's nothing really," said Becky.

"Nothing really?" said Auntie Jem, incredulously. "You call roasted butternut squash with goat's cheese and rocket on a bed of saffron rice, 'nothing really'?"

"Wow!" said Norm's dad. "Sounds absolutely amazing!"

Sounds absolutely gross, thought Norm. What was this supposed to be? Lunch – or some kind of weird reality TV show where contestants had to eat the most disgusting things imaginable?

"Heard from Dad yet?" said Norm's mum to Uncle Steve.

Norm looked up. It was easy to forget that his mum and uncle were actually brother and sister and that Grandpa was his perfect cousins' grandpa too. And if something was easy to forget, Norm usually forgot it.

"Not yet, no," said Uncle Steve.

"Hope he's OK," said Norm's mum.

"Of course he's OK," said Uncle Steve. "He'll ring when he gets there."

"He left his keys for you by the way, love," said Norm's mum.

"What?" said Norm.

"Grandpa?" said Norm's mum. "He left the keys to his shed?"

"Uh?"

"And instructions how to feed the courgettes?"

"Oh, right," said Norm, finally twigging.

That was something else Norm had forgotten. Grandpa was going away for the weekend.

"Oh wow!" said Becky. "I've got this amazing recipe for courgette and banana ice cream!"

But Norm wasn't listening. It was as if he'd been hit slap bang between the eyes by a bolt of lightning – suddenly galvanising his brain into action. Grandpa's shed! Tucked away in a corner of the allotments! The allotments that time had forgotten! Where hardly anyone ever went! What better place to hide a dog?

Norm gathered his thoughts. Or strictly speaking, Norm gathered his *thought*. He only had one. If this was going to work, he was going to need someone to help him. An accomplice. A partner in crime. Not that Norm considered what he was planning to do a crime, of course. As far as Norm was concerned this was a matter of justice being done. A matter of Brian finally getting what he deserved. More importantly, this was a matter of Norm finally getting what *he* deserved too. A dead expensive, bang-up-to-date phone!

Normally, Norm wouldn't have had to think twice who to ask. Mikey would have been the obvious candidate. He and Mikey were best friends. That's what friends were for. Always there for each other. All for one and all that stuff. But Norm was still miffed with Mikey for being so self-centred and unsupportive the other day. OK, so he'd said it was just a joke, but it was no laughing matter as far as Norm was concerned. They hadn't spoken to each other since. Not even on Facebook. Not so much as a text.

"What's up?" said Danny.

"Uh?" said Norm.

"Why are you looking at me like that?"

Until that moment Norm hadn't been aware that he was looking at Danny like anything. Now he was. He was acutely aware. More importantly, Norm knew precisely **why** he was looking at Danny. Danny his so-called **perfect** cousin. Who'd faked his own report. Norm had wondered how that information might be useful to him. Well, he could stop wondering. He knew **exactly** how that information might be useful to him. In fact, never mind **might**. **Would** be useful to him. Why on earth hadn't he thought of it before? It was so screamingly, flippingly obvious!

"Well?" said Danny.

Norm smiled, all of a sudden feeling like the bad guy in a movie. It was all he could do to stop himself throwing his head back and cackling in a suitably evil fashion.

"I'll tell you later."

CHAPTER 24

"You want me to *what*?" said Danny,

"Hide the dog," said Norm, like it was the most natural thing in the world.

"The dog?"

Norm nodded.

"You actually want me to *hide the dog*?" said Danny, articulating each word as if he was talking to a three-year-old and not a nearly thirteen-year-old.

Norm sighed. They'd snuck up to Danny's bedroom after lunch so he could outline the plan. Norm had hoped it would be pretty straightforward. It was turning out to be anything but.

"Why?" said Danny.

"**Because**," said Norm.

"Because what?" persisted Danny.

"**Just because**," said Norm,

glancing anxiously at the door. It could only be a matter of time before someone walked through it.

Danny studied his cousin for a moment. "What's in it for me?" he said, smiling slightly.

"What's in it for *you*?" said Norm.

"Yeah."

It was Norm's turn to smile slightly now. He was going to enjoy this. "I'll tell you what's in it for you, Danny."

"Go on then."

"Your mum and dad not finding out about the faked school report. That's what's in it for you."

Danny's face fell instantly. "I see," he said.

Norm felt a bit bad. It was a pretty drastic threat to make. But desperate times sometimes called for desperate measures. And this was one of those sometimes.

"Have you any idea the pressure I'm under?" said Danny.

Norm pulled a face. "Pressure?" he said. "What pressure's that, then?"

"The pressure of failure," said Danny.

Norm laughed. "Are you winding me up?"

"I'm serious!" said Danny.

"You call one 'B' a failure?" said Norm. *"You got flipping 'As' for everything else!"*

"In my family that's considered a failure," said Danny.

Norm puffed his cheeks out and exhaled

noisily. In **his** family that would be considered a flipping miracle!

"Honestly, you've got no idea what it's like having an older brother and sister who get top marks for everything!" said Danny.

Norm hadn't thought about it like that before. Being the oldest himself, he hadn't *had* to think about it like that before. And if his most recent report was anything to go by, Brian and Dave weren't ever likely to have to think about it either.

"You don't know what it's like to be expected to be the best at everything!" said Danny. "It's tough! Really tough!"

You call **that** tough? thought Norm. Try having your flipping dangleberries plastered all over Facebook! **That's** tough!

"I just want to be..." Danny hesitated, unsure exactly what it was that he just wanted to be.

"Normal?" suggested Norm.

"That's it!" said Danny. "I just want to be normal! Do normal stuff!"

"Eat normal food?" said Norm.

"Exactly!" said Danny. "Play football! Play on the Xbox! Do *nothing* sometimes! Just...you know..." Danny hesitated again, unsure exactly what it was that he just wanted to do.

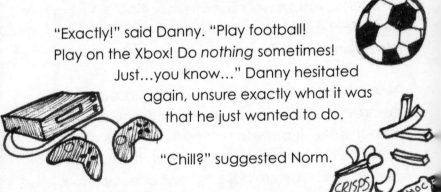

"Chill?" suggested Norm.

"Exactly!" said Danny. "Just chill!"

This was no good, thought Norm. If he wasn't careful, he was going to start feeling sorry for

Danny. And that would never do.

"So?"

"So, what?" said Danny.

"You going to do it, or not? It'll only be for a while. Just till they notice."

Danny looked unsure.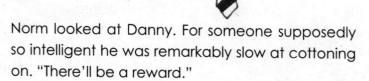

"And then what?"

"They'll stick posters up."

"Then what?"

Norm looked at Danny. For someone supposedly so intelligent he was remarkably slow at cottoning on. "There'll be a reward."

"Right," said Danny.

"So after a while you claim it."

Danny looked puzzled. "How?"

Norm sighed. "What do you mean, how? Isn't it obvious?"

"No," said Danny.

"By pretending to find the flipping dog, that's how!"

"But..." said Danny.

"My dad will cough up the dosh. You give the dosh to me. I don't tell your parents about the report.

And they all lived happily ever after."

"But..."

"But what?" said Norm.

"How do I find the dog if it's lost?"

By now, Norm was beginning to get extremely agitated. Never mind someone walking through the door – if he was up here much longer he was going to have to start shaving.

"It's not **really** going to be lost, Danny."

"What?" said Danny.

"You're going to **hide** the dog, remember?" yelled Norm, finally losing what little patience he had left.

"Norman?" called Norm's mum. "Are you up there?"

Danny and Norm looked at each other. There didn't seem much point denying it. It was pretty obvious Norm *was* up there.

"Come on, love! We're going!"

"Well?" said Norm. "Deal?"

Danny weighed things up for a moment. "Deal," he said reluctantly.

"Excellent," said Norm.

"Where do we hide it?" said Danny.

"I'll tell you tomorrow," said Norm, heading for the door before stopping and turning around. "Can I ask you something?"

"What?" said Danny.

"What did you get the B for?"

"Why do you want to know?"

"Dunno," said Norm. "Just curious."

Danny buried his face in his hands. Merely thinking about it seemed to be a cause of considerable pain and anguish. Like he was about to reveal his darkest most innermost secret from the very depths of his soul. "PE," he said, his voice choked with emotion.

Norm raised his eyebrows. "*PE?*"

Danny nodded, no longer able to even look at

Norm, so great was his shame.

"That's not even a proper subject!" said Norm.

"Try telling my parents that," said Danny.

Norm was beginning to understand just a teensy little bit what it must feel like to be one of his perfect cousins. But he knew he couldn't go there. He couldn't afford to change his mind. He couldn't start feeling sorry for Danny. Not now. There was just too much at stake.

"Norman?" yelled Norm's mum from the foot of the stairs.

"Coming, Mum!" said Norm.

"But..." said Danny.

"I'll be in touch," said Norm, heading off.

CHAPTER 25

The first thing Norm did when he got home later that afternoon was text Danny to tell him to Google 'Polish dog commands' and to be in the park the next morning at ten o'clock. Norm *assumed* Danny didn't already know any Polish dog commands – although when it came to his perfect cousins you just never flipping knew. Norm wouldn't have been in the least bit surprised if they were all fluent in Polish already. In fact, knowing his perfect flipping cousins they probably all went to flipping Polish Dog Command classes already. When they weren't saving the world, or swimming with penguins, or doing flipping capo-flipping-what's-it.

The second thing Norm did when he got home later that afternoon was practise wheelies on the drive. Not that Norm *needed* to practise wheelies. But Norm knew from past experience that if he hung around on the drive at weekends it wouldn't be long before Chelsea appeared on the other side of the fence. And it wasn't.

"Hello, **Norman**."

"Hi," said Norm. Was it *really* a week since Chelsea had last irritated him by saying his name in that really irritating way? But now wasn't the time to let himself get irritated. Now was the time to cut straight to the chase.

"What's the point of that?"

"What's the point of what?" said Norm.

"Riding around on one wheel?" said Chelsea. "Why don't you just get a unicycle?"

It was already proving extremely difficult not to get irritated.

"You could join a circus."

Norm was sorely tempted to tell Chelsea what **she** could do, but thought it best not to.

"I can see you as a clown, *Norman*."

"Really?" said Norm, determined not to rise to the bait.

"Yeah, well, you make *me* laugh, anyway," said Chelsea.

"Glad to hear it," said Norm, tight-lipped.

Chelsea looked at Norm quizzically. Almost as if she was hoping he'd react. Almost like she was disappointed that he *hadn't* reacted.

"Here's the thing," said Norm. "I need you to do something for me."

"Oh, I see!" said Chelsea.

"What do you mean, you **see?**" said Norm.

"*That's* why you're not getting wound up! You're after a favour!"

"Er, yeah. S'pose you could call it a favour, yeah," said Norm.

"Where's your mate?"

"Mikey?"

"Yeah, Mikey. Why don't you ask *him* to do you a favour?"

"I just can't, right?" snapped Norm.

"All right. Keep your hair on, *Norman!*" said Chelsea. "I was only asking!"

They looked at each other for a moment.

"Well, go on then," said Chelsea. "I'm listening."

"I want you to meet me in the park tomorrow morning," said Norm.

Chelsea smiled. "I didn't think you cared."

"What?" said Norm.

flutter flutter

"Sounds like a date to me, *Norman!*"

"It is *not* a date!" said Norm, utterly horrified. Right then Norm couldn't think of anything he'd like less than going on a date with Chelsea. "Not *that* kind of date, anyway!"

"Oh?" said Chelsea, pretending to be hurt. "And what would be so terrible about *that* kind of date?"

What would be so terrible about that? thought Norm. There weren't enough hours in the day to even *begin* to describe what would be so terrible about that. And anyway, thought Norm, he was supposed to be cutting to the chase.

"I need you to..."

"What?" said Chelsea, interjecting. "Protect you?"

Norm sighed. Could Chelsea actually **get** any more annoying? He seriously doubted it.

"No," said Norm. "I need you to distract my brothers."

"Distract them?"

"Just for a couple of minutes."

"Why?" said Chelsea.

"That's for you to know and me to find out," said Norm.

Chelsea pulled a face.

"Look, I just need you to do it, right?" said Norm. "You don't need to know why."

Chelsea studied Norm for a few seconds. Norm had a funny feeling he knew what was coming next. And he was absolutely right.

"What's in it for me?"

"You can keep the twenty pounds," said Norm.

"What twenty pounds?" said Chelsea.

"The twenty pounds I said you could keep if you didn't post the photo on Facebook."

Chelsea shrugged. "I've already spent it."

"But..."

"And I already posted the photo."

"Yeah," said Norm. "About that."

"What about it?" said Chelsea.

Norm didn't know what to say. What **could** he say? Chelsea **had** posted the photo. The damage had already been done. And in the great scheme of things he could afford to kiss goodbye to the twenty pounds. With luck he'd soon have considerably more than that in his back pocket. As long as everything went to plan.

"Will you do it anyway?" asked Norm sheepishly.

Chelsea hesitated. "I might."

Might was OK, thought Norm. He could live with *might*. It was better than an outright no. And it wasn't like he had much choice. Brian and Dave would have to be distracted somehow while Danny tried to lure John away.

Norm couldn't believe it. He'd called the dog John! OK, so only in his head and not actually out loud. But even so. This was no time to start getting attached. This was no time to start getting sentimental. This was the time to be ruthless and cold-hearted. It was just a stupid flipping dog. A stupid flipping dog with a stupid flipping name.

"Go on," said Norm.

Chelsea smiled. "What do you say?"

Norm sighed. This was going to hurt. But some things had to be done. And this was one of them.

"*Please*," muttered Norm under his breath.

"I can't hear you," said Chelsea, relishing the moment.

Norm gritted his teeth. **"Please,"** he said.

"That's better," said Chelsea. "What time?"

"Ten o'clock," said Norm, visibly brightening. "So you'll do it, then?"

Chelsea smiled again. "I might," she said, before turning and walking away.

Norm watched her go. One day Chelsea was going to pay. For posting the photo. For keeping the money. For saying his name in that funny way. For generally being

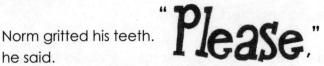

annoying. Just not today though. Or even tomorrow.

Tomorrow it was Brian's turn.

CHAPTER 26

And so it was that Norm found himself heading to the park – with his two little brothers and their dog named after his grandpa's favourite member of The Beatles – just before ten o'clock on Sunday morning. Luckily his suggestion that he accompany Brian and Dave hadn't raised any eyebrows. Norm's mum had been too busy flicking round shopping channels at the time and had barely even registered Norm walking into the room, let alone what he'd actually said. Norm's dad, meanwhile, had still been in bed, snoring like a baby. A baby rhinoceros, that is. With constipation.

Norm's suggestion to go on a walk hadn't surprised Brian or Dave either, as strictly speaking Norm wasn't actually *going* for a walk himself – he was going for a bike ride. Not that it meant getting to the park any quicker.

"Could you two *go* any slower?"

"I dunno," said Dave. "We could try."

Norm wobbled slightly. If *he* went any flipping slower he'd fall off.

"What's the hurry, anyway?" said Brian.

Norm had to think quickly on his feet. Or rather, on his pedals.

"It's going to rain."

"Really?" said Brian doubtfully. "Doesn't look like it."

Brian was right. It didn't look like it was going to rain.

"There aren't any clouds," said Dave, looking up at the bright blue sky.

234

Dave was right. There weren't any clouds.

"Global warming," said Norm.

"Global warming?" said Brian. "What are you talking about?"

Norm had absolutely no idea what he was talking about. All he knew was that if they didn't get a shift on they'd be late for their rendezvous with Chelsea. Not that his brothers knew about their rendezvous with Chelsea of course. It had to appear as spontaneous and unplanned as possible.

"Why don't you let John have a run round?" suggested Norm as they finally reached the park with just a couple of minutes to spare.

"Good idea," said Brian, unclipping the lead from the dog's collar.

But instead of having a run around, the dog celebrated its new-found freedom by sitting down and licking itself in the nether regions.

"Imagine being able to do that," said Dave.

"I'd rather not if you don't mind," said Brian.

Norm scanned the horizon before eventually spotting a speck in the distance running towards them. Could that be who he thought it was? Could that be who he *hoped* it was? His knight in shining armour? Or whatever a girl knight was called, anyway.

"Hey, look!" said Norm. "It's Chelsea!"

Brian and Dave looked in the direction that Norm was looking.

"Where?" said Brian. "I can't see her."

"How do you know that's Chelsea?" said Dave. "It's just a speck."

Good point, thought Norm. Perhaps he should've waited till the speck had got a little bit bigger before saying anything.

"I just do, right?"

"You've got good eyesight, Norman," said Dave.

"Carrots," said Norm.

"What?" said Dave.

"Carrots,"
repeated Norm.
"Good for your eyesight."

Brian pulled a face. "I thought carrots helped you see in the dark."

"No, Brian," said Norm. "That's torches. *Torches* help you see in the dark."

"Uh?" said Brian.

Norm peered and squinted, holding a hand over his eyes to shield them from the glare of the morning sun. It was definitely Chelsea! She'd come after all!

"Hey, guys!" she panted, running up and stopping.

"Hi," sang Brian and Dave, together.

"Hello, *Norman*," said Chelsea smiling. "Fancy seeing you here."

"Yeah, fancy," said Norm.

"Do you come here often?"

"Not really."

"Me neither," said Chelsea. "What are the odds, eh?"

"Of what?" said Norm.

"You and me both being here at the same time. In the park. Ten o'clock on a Sunday morning!"

"Yeah," said Norm. "Pretty random."

"No, not random, *Norman*," said Chelsea. "Fate! That's what it is!"

"Fate?" said Norm.

"Oh, definitely," said Chelsea. "It's almost like it was *meant* to happen."

Norm glared at Chelsea. Much more of this and she was going to give the flipping game away.

"What?" said Dave, immediately sensing that something was going on.

"Nothing," said Norm.

"Why did you look at Chelsea like that?"

"I didn't look at her like anything."

"Yeah you did," said Dave. "I saw you."

Norm glared at his youngest brother.

"Just like that!" said Dave.

"I don't know what you're talking about, Dave."

But both Norm and Dave knew exactly what Dave

was talking about. For a seven-year-old, Dave was very sharp. He never missed a trick – and it looked like he hadn't missed this one.

"You going for a run then?" said Brian, changing the subject so that Norm didn't have to bother.

"Course she's going for a run, you doughnut! What does it *look* like she's doing? Flying a flipping kite?"

"She might have lost it," said Dave.

"Lost what?" said Norm.

"Her kite," said Dave.

"Shut up, Dave, you little freak!" hissed Norm.

"That's not a very nice way to talk to your brother," said Chelsea.

"He's my flipping brother!" said Norm. "I'll talk to him how I flipping want!"

"Ooooh!" said Chelsea sarcastically, before turning to Brian and Dave. "I think someone's overtired, don't you?"

Brian and Dave burst into gales of laughter, conveniently drowning out a muffled voice from behind a nearby bush.

"Domnie," hissed the voice. "Domnie."

"I am **not** over-flipping-tired!" yelled Norm.

Chelsea frowned. "Over-flipping-tired? Is that even a proper word, *Norman*?"

Norm tried to think. What exactly **was** it about Chelsea that he found so flipping annoying? And then he remembered. Everything. That was it. He found *everything* about Chelsea so flipping annoying.

"Where's John?" said Brian.

"What?" said Norm.

"Where's John?" repeated Brian, a note of panic beginning to creep into his voice.

Norm looked round. Sure enough, there was no sign of the dog.

"John?" shouted Brian. "Here, boy!"

But John was nowhere to be seen or heard. It was as if he'd suddenly vanished into thin air.

Chelsea caught Norm's eye and tilted her head ever so slightly. But it was enough. In that one instant the penny suddenly dropped. Norm suddenly twigged. Chelsea had done it on purpose. She'd *deliberately* wound him up to distract his brothers like Norm had wanted her to. And while his brothers had been distracted, Danny had snuck off with the dog! Respect where respect was due, thought Norm grudgingly. As painful as it was for him to admit it, it was genius. No other word for it. Sheer flipping genius.

"Oh, I see," said Chelsea, putting two and two together.

"What?" said Brian.

"Nothing," said Norm quickly. "Come on, guys. We'd better get looking."

"What for?" said Dave.

"John, of course!" said Norm.

Dave raised an eyebrow. "Perhaps it's already too late," he said.

"What do you mean, too late?" said Brian. "Don't say that, Dave!"

Clearly traumatised, Brian began to sob softly. Excellent, thought Norm. See how *he* flipping likes it. OK, so in terms of actual trauma suffered, losing some stupid dog hardly compared to being plastered all over Facebook stark flipping naked – but even so, it was good to see Brian finally suffering like Norm had been doing. It had been a long time coming, but revenge was just as sweet – if not even sweeter.

"I don't mean too late as in – you know – *too late*," said Dave.

"Well, what *do* you mean, then?" sniffed Brian.

"I mean perhaps it's too late to bother looking," said Dave.

"What?" said Brian, getting more upset by the second.

"Perhaps it's time to go home and make a few posters."

Dave looked knowingly at Norm.

"I *see*," said Chelsea, looking at Dave looking knowingly at Norm. "You coming, *Norman*?"

"What?" said Norm. "Where to?"

"To make posters, of course," said Chelsea.

"Er, no," said Norm suddenly realising that Danny had absolutely no idea where he was supposed to be taking the dog to. "I've just remembered something."

"Oh yeah?" said Chelsea. "And what's that?"

"I've got to feed my grandpa's courgettes."

"A likely story," grinned Chelsea.

"What?" said Norm.

"Is that really the best you can do?" said Chelsea. "You've got to feed your grandpa's courgettes?"

"No, really I have," said Norm. "Do you think you could take my brothers home for me?"

Chelsea looked at Norm, clearly weighing up the situation.

"No problem," she said eventually.

"Thanks," yelled Norm, setting off on his bike in the direction of the allotments. "I owe you one!"

"You owe me more than one, **_Norman!_**" yelled Chelsea, watching him go.

CHAPTER 27

"Here, boy," said Norm, unlocking Grandpa's shed and attempting to usher John inside.

John sat down.

"Shift," said Norm.

John showed no sign whatsoever of shifting and instead started scratching himself vigorously behind one ear.

Norm sighed. "Stupid flipping dog."

"He's not stupid," said Danny. "He's Polish, remember?"

"Oh yeah," said Norm. "Silly me. Fancy forgetting we had a Polish dog."

"**Donnie**," said Danny,

disappearing inside the shed. John instantly sprang to his feet and trotted happily after him.

Norm followed Danny and the dog into Grandpa's shed and closed the door. So far so good. Everything was going according to plan. But it was important not to be seen. Things could still go horribly wrong.

"So what now?" said Danny.

"Give it a couple of hours and then call," said Norm.

"A couple of hours?" said Danny.

"Got to at least give them time to make the posters," said Norm.

"Yeah, suppose so," said Danny.

"You can't phone before they've even stuck them up."

"Hadn't thought of that," said Danny.

"And anyway," said Norm, "you've got to disguise yourself."

"Why?" said Danny.

"Isn't it obvious?"

One look at Danny's face told Norm that it was far from obvious.

"They can't know it's **you**, Danny, you doughnut!" said Norm getting more and more exasperated.

"They'll know it's a flipping set-up, won't they?"

Danny pulled a face. "But they'll know it's me when I start to talk."

"Not if you put on a funny voice, they won't!"

Gordon flipping Bennet, thought Norm, looking at his so-called perfect cousin and shaking his head in despair. How Danny had managed to get a near-perfect report was a mystery to him. He might be good at maths and English and history and all that boring stuff, but when it came to more practical matters like how to pull off a decent scam he hadn't got a flipping clue.

"That's brilliant!" said Danny.

"No, it's not," said Norm. "It's common **Flipping** sense, *that's* what it is."

Danny studied Norm for a moment. "And you won't tell?"

"Won't tell what?" said Norm.

"My mum and dad," said Danny. "About me faking my report?"

Norm didn't reply immediately, choosing instead to savour the moment and keep Danny in suspense for just a little bit longer. And besides, he'd just remembered something. He was supposed to be feeding Grandpa's courgettes.

"Your secret's safe with me, Danny," said Norm, reading the instructions Grandpa had left.

Danny smiled gratefully.

"As long as you don't mess up."

CHAPTER 28

Norm was busy browsing phones on the net when he heard the tell-tale creak of the creaky floorboard. He didn't bother looking round to see who it was. He didn't need to. He already knew.

"Hi, Dave."

"Hi," said Dave, unsurprised that Norm was unsurprised. He knew that Norm would know who it was.

"So?" said Norm, swivelling round in his chair.

"What?" said Dave.

"Come on, Dave. Don't play the innocent. Just get it over with. It'll save a lot of time."

Youngest and oldest brother looked at each other for a moment, each secretly hoping and wishing that middle brother wouldn't suddenly turn up. There was stuff to talk about. In private.

"I want in," said Dave.

"What do you mean?" said Norm, even though he knew perfectly well what Dave meant. He thought he'd check anyway. Just in case. Make sure they were singing off the same hymn sheet or whatever that expression was.

"**50/50**," said Dave.

Norm was gobsmacked. He'd expected Dave to want a cut of the so-called 'reward' money. But **50/50?** He was having a flipping laugh!

"**Are you serious?**"

Dave smiled. He was serious all right.

"And if I don't agree?" said Norm.

But Norm already knew the answer. It was pretty flipping obvious. If he didn't agree, Dave would tell his parents everything. How the whole thing had been a set-up. How the dog hadn't really been *lost* at all.

"Where is he?"

"Who?" said Norm. "Brian? Making the posters, isn't he?"

"I meant John," said Dave.

"That's for me to know and you to find out," said Norm, finally getting it right.

"Grandpa's shed," Dave shot back.

Norm sighed. "So why flipping ask then?"

"I was just checking."

Dave looked at the PC screen. "Do you know which one you're going to get yet?"

"Well, it's going to have to be a cheaper one now, isn't it?"

"Not necessarily," said Dave.

Norm pulled a face. "What do you mean, not necessarily?"

Dave shrugged. "We could come to some sort of...arrangement?"

Norm was beginning to get frustrated. Actually, Norm had already become frustrated. He was beginning to get *extremely* frustrated. And it was surely only a matter of time before they got interrupted. They were already pushing their luck.

"Arrangement?" said Norm.

"I'll lend you the rest of the money."

Norm pulled another face. He was having trouble getting his head round this. "You'll *lend* me the money that I'm going to **give** you?"

"The  money, yeah," said Dave, making speech marks in the air. "Plus interest, of course."

"Interest?" said Norm.

"Well, you don't think I'm going to do it for free, do you?" said Dave.

Norm couldn't believe it. He was being given a taste of his own medicine by a flipping seven-year-old!

"Dave?" yelled Brian from the bottom of the stairs.

"Yeah?" said Dave.

"We need to go out and put the posters up!"

"Coming," said Dave.

Norm and Dave looked at each other.

"Deal?" said Dave.

Norm thought for a moment. There really wasn't much to think about. Not if he wanted that dead expensive bang-up-to-date phone.

"Deal."

"Excellent," said Dave, turning to leave before stopping again. "Oh, and one more thing."

"What?" said Norm.

"You promised me your old phone, remember?"

"What?" said Norm again.

"You promised me your old phone."

"I did?" said Norm.

"When I was 'sleepwalking' the other night?" said Dave – making speech marks in the air again. "Unless of course you want Dad to know how he ended up with that rash on his face?"

Norm couldn't help smiling. You had to hand it to Dave. He was good. He was very good.

CHAPTER 29

Brian and Dave were scarcely back through the door before the phone rang. Norm's mum picked up.

"Hello?"

Norm looked at his mum anxiously. Or at least he *tried* to look at his mum anxiously. He had a pretty good idea who it was already. And what it would be about.

"You've got him? Oh, that's wonderful!"

Beaming broadly, Norm's mum gave Brian and Dave the thumbs-up. Brian immediately whooped and started to dance round the kitchen. Dave followed suit a fraction of a second later – and fractionally less convincingly.

"Thank you so much!" said Norm's mum. "I'll just give you our add—"

Norm's mum stopped mid-sentence and pulled a face. "That's funny."

"What's the matter, Mum?" said Brian, instantly worried again.

"They hung up before I could give them the address," said Norm's mum, putting the phone back down.

"Idiot," muttered Norm under his breath.

"What was that, Norman?" said Norm's dad, looking up from his paper.

"Er, nothing," said Norm quickly. "I was just thinking. What an idiot. How will he know where to come if he doesn't know the address?"

"He?" said Norm's mum, raising an eyebrow.

"What?" said Norm.

"You said *he*, love. How do you know it was a *he*?"

"Erm, just a guess," said Norm.

"**50/50**," said Dave.

"Shut up, Dave!" hissed Norm.

"I just meant it was a **50/50** chance of it being a he," said Dave.

"Oh, right," said Norm.

You could have cut the tension with a knife. If Norm hadn't already blown it, he had now.

"What did you *think* Dave meant?" said Norm's dad, narrowing his eyes and fixing Norm with a particularly steely stare.

"Nothing," said Norm.

"Come on, love," said Norm's mum gently. "What's going on?"

The game was up and Norm knew it. Norm's mum and dad knew it. Dave knew it. There was only one person who *didn't* know it.

"I want John back!" wailed Brian, suddenly bursting into floods of tears.

Norm looked at his middle brother for a moment. If it hadn't been for Brian giving Chelsea the photo in the first flipping place, none of this would have had to flipping well happen. Norm wouldn't have been forced to take such drastic action. It was all Brian's flipping fault. He'd only got himself to blame.

Why then was Norm beginning to experience strange stirrings and weird feelings? Feelings that he couldn't quite explain? But feelings of what?

Sympathy? Sympathy for his *brother*? Surely not, thought Norm. That couldn't be right. Or could it? Brian had been on an emotional rollercoaster lately. An emotional rollercoaster that Norm knew only too well. One minute you were up and the next you were down.

That's what it was! thought Norm. He knew *exactly* how Brian felt! It was *so* flipping annoying!

"Don't worry, you'll get him back," said Norm.

"But he doesn't know where we live!" gulped Brian.

"Oh, yes, he does," said Norm.

"How do you know?" said Brian.

Norm glanced at his mum and dad. "I just flipping do, right?"

CHAPTER 30

"Suppose we start at the beginning?" said Norm's dad once Brian and Dave had gone outside to await John's imminent arrival.

Suppose we *don't*, thought Norm, who had no intention of discussing the Facebook photo ever again if he could possibly help it. He'd suffered more humiliation already than most people suffered in a flipping lifetime. It was time to draw a line underneath it. Two lines even. In ink. In fact, never mind ink, thought Norm. Flipping felt tip.

"So who was that on the phone?" said Norm's dad. "Mikey?"

Norm seriously wished it *had* been Mikey on the phone. Because if it **had** been Mikey on the phone, Mikey wouldn't have made such a basic error. If it **had** been Mikey on the phone it wouldn't have all gone pear-shaped. They wouldn't have been having this flipping conversation now.

"Danny," said Norm.

"Danny?" said Norm's mum in amazement.

Norm nodded.

"But..."

"What, Mum? You thought he was perfect?"

"Don't try and shift the blame, Norman," said Norm's dad.

"But..." began Norm.

"And don't answer back!"

Norm sighed.

"And you can pack **that** in as well."

"What?"

"Sighing," said Norm's dad.

There was a sudden
commotion outside.
A mixture of excited
yelling and excited
yelping. John was back.

"Why did you do it, love?" said Norm's mum.

Norm thought for a moment. What could he say?
What *should* he say? That it was all a matter of
revenge? That he wanted to quite deliberately
traumatise Brian in order to pay him back for all the
grief *he'd* been through? Would his parents even
begin to understand it? Norm seriously doubted it.

"I needed the money, Mum."

"What for?" said Norm's mum.

"Let me guess," said Norm's dad. "A new phone?"

Norm nodded sheepishly.

"Do you not think I'd have noticed?"

Honestly? thought Norm. Not a chance. But then Norm doubted whether his dad would have noticed if his own socks were on fire, never mind whether Norm had got a flipping new phone or not. But Norm chose not to say anything. The sooner this was over the better.

"Do you think we're stupid, Norman?" continued Norm's dad.

Again, Norm thought it better not to say anything.

"We can't afford the reward money, love," said Norm's mum.

"How much is it?" said Norm.

Of course it was all hypothetical. Norm knew he wouldn't be getting the money now – but he was curious to know precisely how *much* he wouldn't be getting now.

Norm's dad raised an eyebrow. "You mean, was it?"

Norm nodded.

"Twenty pounds," said Norm's dad.

" *Twenty pounds?* " blurted Norm.

" *Is that all?* "

The room suddenly went very quiet.

"I mean – *was* that all?" said Norm, correcting himself before anyone else could.

"Was that *all*?" said Norm's dad.

"Yeah." Norm had been hoping to get a dead expensive, bang-up-to-date phone with the reward money. But twenty pounds? He'd have been lucky to get a flipping **cover** for a phone for *that* – never mind an actual flipping phone! It was just as well he wasn't going to get it now. Twenty pounds? Frankly it was an insult! Actually, it was an insult to the flipping dog! His parents were such skinflints!

"It was all we could afford, love," said Norm's mum gently. "We couldn't bear the thought of your brothers being upset."

Flipping typical, thought Norm. Never mind *him*. As long his precious little brothers weren't upset. *That* was the main thing.

The door suddenly burst open and in rushed John, followed by Brian and Dave and eventually by a figure wearing a baseball cap and what appeared to be a false nose, a false moustache and false glasses.

"Look, everyone!" yelled Brian, almost beside himself with excitement. "It's John!"

John barked dutifully.

"Hello, Danny," said Norm's mum.

"Great disguise," muttered Norm.

"Sorry," said Danny.

Norm's mum smiled and shook her head.

"Are you going to tell my parents, Auntie Linda?"

Norm's mum and dad looked at each other. *Were* they? There hadn't been a chance to talk about this yet.

"About the report, I mean," said Danny.

"Report?" said Norm's mum.

"Oh, I thought..." began Danny, before noticing that Norm was glaring at him. Norm hadn't got round to telling his mum and dad that bit yet. He wasn't even sure he was *going* to tell his mum and dad that bit. Not just now anyway. It could still prove valuable information sometime in the future.

"What's going on?" said Norm's dad, the vein on the side of his head beginning to throb. Unlike Norm, John spotted it immediately and without warning, leapt onto Norm's dad's lap and began licking it.

"Get off me!" said Norm's dad.

"He's Polish," said Norm, only too happy to change the subject. "He can't understand you, Dad."

"What?" said Norm's dad doubtfully. "Polish?"

"Domnie," said Danny.

John immediately stopped licking Norm's dad and obediently trotted over to Danny.

"Dobry pies," said Danny. "Dobry pies."

"Well, well," said Norm's dad. "That'll save a few quid in dog-training classes!"

"Yes, well done, Danny!" said Norm's mum.

Yes, well done, **Danny**, thought Norm bitterly. Never mind the fact that Danny was just as involved in the reward-money scam as he was, all of a sudden Danny was the flipping blue-eyed boy again! Flipping typical!

Norm's dad stroked his chin thoughtfully for a few seconds. "I don't think there's any need to tell your parents, Danny, do you?"

"Really?" said Danny, hardly daring to believe what he was hearing.

"It's pretty obvious Norman put you up to this," said Norm's dad. "He has previous experience when it comes to this kind of thing. Don't you, Norman?"

"Hey, what can I say?" said Norm, who, despite being in big trouble, couldn't help feeling just a teensy bit proud of himself. It might not be the greatest reputation in the world to have, but at least it was a reputation.

"How about 'sorry', love?" said Norm's mum.

"Exactly," said Norm's dad. "At least Danny had the decency to apologise."

This constant big-upping of Danny was seriously beginning to do Norm's head in. As far as Norm was concerned Danny was just as guilty as he was – if not more.

"Sorry," muttered Norm.

"I should think so too," said Norm's dad. "Now, about this new phone."

Norm glanced at Danny.

"I thought you said you weren't into phones?"

said Danny.

"Yeah, well, you know," said Norm.

"You're going to have to earn this money, Norman," said Norm's dad.

Norm looked completely and utterly horrified. Had his dad really just said what he thought he'd said? He was going to have to **earn** the money? **Earn** it? Like, actually *do* something? He'd need to check with Danny later, but he was pretty sure slavery had been abolished.

"Earn it, Dad? How?"

"By doing chores around the house, love," said Norm's mum.

"**Chores?**" said Norm, pulling a face like he'd just sucked on a piece of lemon.

"And errands."

This was getting worse by the flipping second, thought Norm. Chores and errands? What was this? Medieval times or something?

"And generally improving your attitude and behaviour," said Norm's dad.

"But…" said Norm.

"Now give me your phone."

Norm stared at his dad in disbelief.

"What?"

"You heard, Norman. Give me your phone."

"Why?"

"Because I say so, that's why!"

274

"It's your punishment, love," said Norm's mum.

" **That is so unfair!** "
blurted Norm, handing over his phone.

"You can have mine if you want," said Danny.

Norm's mum and dad turned and stared at Danny.

"Er, once you've been allowed your own phone back, I mean."

Norm pulled a face. "But you've only just got it."

"I know," said Danny. "But my parents have said they'll get me another one."

"How come?" said Norm.

Danny looked a bit sheepish.

"Capoeira."

Norm's mum and dad looked at Danny blankly.

"It's a Brazilian art form that combines elements of martial arts, sports and music, created by descendants of African slaves in the sixteenth century," said Danny.

"Right," said Norm's dad, clearly impressed.

"There was a competition yesterday," said Danny.

"And?" said Norm's mum expectantly.

"I won," said Danny.

Course you flipping did, thought Norm, heading for the door. He'd had enough. There was someone he needed to see. Someone normal. Someone who was less than perfect. Someone who didn't know what capo-flipping-eira was.

"Where do you think you're going?" said Norm's dad.

"Mikey's," said Norm without bothering to turn round.

"Hilarious stuff from one of my comic heroes!" Harry Hill

THE WORLD OF
NORM
MAY CONTAIN NUTS

Jonathan Meres

Norman knew it was going to be one of those days when he woke up and found himself about to pee in his dad's wardrobe.

Why on earth did Norm's family have to move, anyway? In their old house he'd never tried to pee in anything other than a toilet. And when Norm is in bed, he's kept awake by his dad snoring like a constipated rhinoceros! Will life ever get less unfair for Norm?

978 1 40831 303 9 £5.99 PB
978 1 40831 579 8 £4.99 eBook

ORCHARD BOOKS
Celebrating 25 Years
www.orchardbooks.co.uk

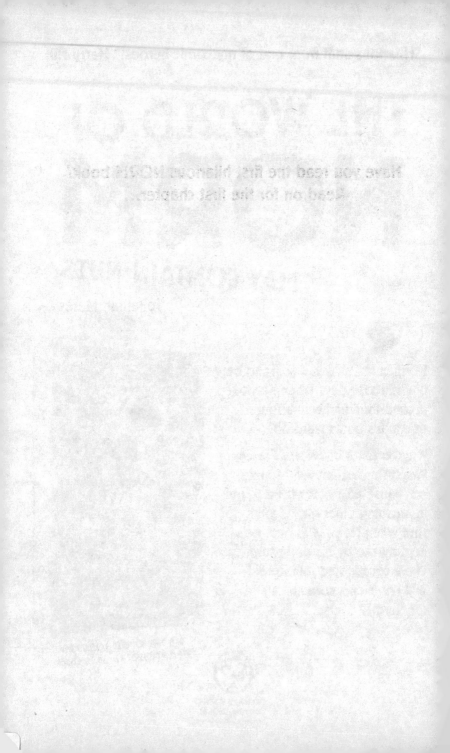

Have you read the first hilarious NORM book?
Read on for the first chapter…

CHAPTER 1

Norm knew it was going to be one of those days when he woke up and found himself about to pee in his dad's wardrobe.

"Whoa! Stop Norman!" yelled Norm's dad, sitting bolt upright and switching on his bedside light.

"Uh? What?" mumbled Norm, his voice still thick with sleep.

"What do you think you're doing?"

"Having a pee?" said Norm, like this was the most stupid question in the entire history of stupid questions.

"Not in my wardrobe you're not!" said Norm's dad.

"That's from Ikea that is," added Norm's mum, like it was somehow OK to pee in a wardrobe that wasn't.

Norm was confused. The last thing he knew he'd been on the verge of becoming the youngest ever World Mountain Biking Champion, when he'd suddenly had to slam on his brakes to avoid hitting a tree. Now here he was having to slam on a completely different kind of brakes in order to avoid a completely different kind of accident. What was going on? And what were his parents doing sleeping in the bathroom anyway?

"Toilet's moved," said Norm, hopping from one foot to the other, something which at the age of three was considered socially acceptable, but which at the age of nearly thirteen, most definitely wasn't.

"What?" said Norm's dad.

"Toilet's moved," said Norm, a bit louder.

But Norm's dad had heard what
Norm said. He just couldn't
quite *believe* what Norm
had said.

"No, Norman. It's not the *toilet*
that's moved! It's *us* that's moved!"

"Forgot," said Norm.

Norm's dad looked at his eldest son. "Are you
serious?"

"Yeah," said Norm, like this was the *second* most
stupid question in the entire history of stupid
questions.

"You *forgot* we moved house?"

"Yeah," said Norm.

"How can you *forget* we moved house?" said Norm's dad, increasingly incredulous.

"Just did," shrugged Norm, increasingly close to wetting himself.

"But we moved over three months ago, Norman!" said Norm's dad.

"Three months, two weeks and five days ago, to be precise," said Norm's mum, like she hadn't even had to think about it.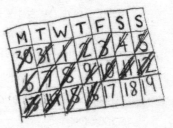

Norm's dad sighed wearily and looked at his watch. It was two o'clock in the morning.

"Look, Norman. You just can't go round peeing in other peoples' wardrobes and that's all there is to it!"

"I didn't," said Norm.

"No, but you were *about* to!"

Norm's dad was right. Norm *had* been about to pee in the wardrobe, but he'd managed to stop himself just in time.

Typical, thought Norm. Being blamed for something he hadn't actually done.

Norm considered arguing the point, but by now his bladder felt like it was the size of a space hopper. If he didn't pee soon he was going to explode. Then he'd *really* be in trouble!

"Go on. Clear off," said Norm's dad.

Norm didn't need telling twice and began waddling towards the door like a pregnant penguin.

"Oh, and Norman?"

"Yeah?" said Norm without bothering to stop.

"The toilet's at the end of the corridor. You can't miss it."

Norm didn't reply. He knew that if he didn't get to the toilet in the next ten seconds there was a very good chance that he *would* miss it!